The Hope
The Prayer
The Anthem

The Hope
The Prayer
The Anthem

An Anthology

Published by Afritondo Media and Publishing 2021

First published in Great Britain in 2021
by Afritondo Media and Publishing
Preston, United Kingdom
www.afritondo.com

ISBN: 9781838027926

For all those who seek to find themselves

CONTENTS

We do not inherit the earth from our ancestors; we borrow it from our children.

African proverb

SILLY NELSON
Athol Williams

Mama said I was being foolish going there. She didn't try to stop me though. She never stops me from doing things. That's not her way. She'd rather mock me and send me out feeling more unsure of my beliefs than usual.

She often referred to me as a silly boy. On occasion, with venom on her tongue, she'd go further: 'You're just a fat, bald, silly boy, Nelson.' Always in her sweet voice, never shouting. I'd remind her that at thirty-seven I was not a boy, that I was a grown man.

She'd never say it, but I knew she was glad that I never left home, that she got to have me around all these years. At least I had a job and contributed to our home, otherwise she'd have been unable to pay the rent.

I'd been fired from both my previous jobs. At the hospital, they said I committed fraud by admitting patients who couldn't pay. Turning away mothers with sick children just because they couldn't afford the hospital bills seemed ridiculous to me. So I found a way around the patients admission system and admitted them. When I worked at the grocery store as a teller, it broke my heart to see people remove items from their trolleys, before I rang them up, because they didn't have enough money. I'd pack the items in their bags without scanning. I knew it was against the rules but helping people in need seemed more important.

'Why did you do that? Why do you have to be so silly!' Mama said each time I came home with news that I'd lost my job. She'd speak in her condescending tone like I was a little puppy who had made a mess in the living room.

I acknowledge doing something once that I agree was silly: I saw a group of men working hard, loading furniture from a house into a truck, so offered to lend a hand. I later learned that I had abetted a burglary.

Mama's view was that the world was a tough place and that I needed to toughen up. By this, she meant that I was not to care about others. To me, that was foolish or silly. Still, being called foolish and silly hurt. These are heavy words—words that press down on your head, in that dent on your skull where your deepest insecurities swirl with your beliefs. That was all I had, insecurities and beliefs.

My belief in people took me to the prison that autumn afternoon to meet a young woman convicted of murder.

'Why would you go see that evil woman?' Mama said when I told her. It was more a taunt than a question. And she didn't say 'woman'; she used an offensive word sometimes used to refer to women, a word that I hate. I tried to explain that there were no evil people only evil acts, that we each had equal propensity to do good or evil, that it was our circumstances that pushed us one way or the other. 'Rubbish,' she said, waving a dismissive hand at me like she was swatting a fly. 'People are either good or evil, Nelson. That's just the way it is. And prisons, prisons are filled with only one kind—evil people.'

I couldn't comprehend Mama's hardness, her unwillingness or inability to show compassion. She irritated me with adages like 'no good deed goes unpunished' whenever I helped someone. From what I could tell, the world needed more good deeds, so I persisted.

'If people are either good or evil, then which am I?' I asked her.

'You're just silly, Nelson,' she replied, 'just a silly boy.'

I'd read about Flo Maisela's case online. She was a nineteen-year-old woman who had stabbed a man to death at a party. It was not the murder that caused public outrage but the fact that her trial had lasted only an hour. Human rights groups went berserk. They claimed that Flo had been denied a fair trial. How could it only take an hour for a court to find someone guilty of murder and then sentence them to death?

With a broken beer bottle, Flo had stabbed the man repeatedly. Witnesses saw her covered in his blood. DNA tests were conclusive. And she pleaded guilty. These were all revealed in the whirlwind trial. The media reminded us that the victim died in less than an hour. 'We've given her more than she deserves,' they concluded.

At four minutes before three, I took a seat in a bleak room at Greystoke Women's Prison, waiting to meet Flo, the murderer. I'd never met someone who'd taken a life. Where would I meet such a person anyway? Certainly not at home among Mama's friends.

The visitors' room was stark and uninviting. The walls looked like they were painted blue a long time ago. The concrete floor was shiny around the perimeter—perhaps where no feet had ever walked—but was mostly stripped of its varnish, leaving the floor raw and rough. There were two dirty white plastic chairs at opposite ends of the small room. I sat in one. I hate those chairs. I can't relax in them, always worrying that they're going to shatter under my weight and I'll be impaled by a large plastic stake. The room had no window to the outside, only a window in the metal door that gave a view of the corridor. The room was lit by a single fluorescent tube. Standard local prison stock, I imagined.

I can still picture myself there: I'm sitting with my back against one of the walls of the square room, the door to my right; the other chair is against the opposite wall about five paces away. I'd wondered if this was deliberate, that the warders chose to place the prisoner as far away as possible from the visitor. Or perhaps this was the distance the previous occupants of the room wanted. Perhaps it was fear that sent the previous visitor as far away as he could get from the person in the other chair. The same fear that fuelled Mama's nastiness that morning. She wanted to know if there'd be a barrier between me and the murderer, if there'd be a guard in the room and who else would be present. I had no answers. I hadn't asked any of these questions when I set up the meeting with Flo. What I did know was that I was going because Flo's mother had asked me to.

There was movement at the door. I turned to my right but no one entered, just people walking along the corridor. Flo's mother suggested that I arrange to go to the prison that specific day at three in the afternoon because that was teatime for the prisoners. It seemed so civilized that prisoners had teatime. I wondered if they actually got tea or if this was just a remnant of bygone days, a remnant that has become a label.

I looked across to the other chair. I pictured Flo sitting there, a frightened little girl thrust into an ugly world. A person Mama would regard as evil because she'd broken 'God's commandment', yet Mama broke God's commandments all the time.

I got up slowly, walked over to the other chair, and brought it slightly closer to mine. I took my seat again; that felt better. But the tension in my chest didn't feel good at all. I could feel it rising as I sat waiting. I had no idea what I was going to say to the prisoner when she arrived. Flo's mother said she'd watched a YouTube video I'd recorded about humanity and love. Usually, the videos of my mumbo-jumbo, as Mama calls it, get no attention, but this one went viral. Flo's mother found me on Facebook and sent a message introducing herself and telling me about her daughter. She asked if I would go see Flo. I'd asked why. She said my video moved her to make the request, that she believed a visit from me would ease her daughter's pain.

The video had gone viral for the wrong reasons: I talked about loving whites. A black man talking about loving white people caused a massive stir among black people who thought it absurd. At a time when blacks around the world were standing up to centuries of white oppression, when black people were fighting for equality before the law and fighting to be treated with dignity, the last thing they wanted to hear was that we should love whites. I talked about the need to affirm each other's humanity before seeking to address our conflicts and pain. I talked about loving the other person even as they were punching us in the face. This was what our humanity demanded.

The video earned me comments of hatred and threats. People commented that I suffered from Stockholm syndrome, that I was a coconut, brown on the outside and white on the inside, that I was still enslaved and was pandering to my white masters. Mama was upset: 'Look what you've done now. You've gone and angered everyone. People are calling you all sorts of names, even racist. I'm getting messages from my friends, asking me what's wrong with you. How could you say such stupid things?'

'Should we not love white people?' I asked her.

'That's not the point,' she spat back.

'I believe we all yearn to have our humanity affirmed, to be seen, not looked through. To have our fears, pains, and dreams acknowledged. Frankly, that's all I've ever wanted, Mama.'

She hadn't said anything, but I could hear her mocking me, calling me all sorts of horrible names. Talking about love had angered people and earned me the label, racist.

'Is she black or white?'

'Who?'

'This woman you're seeing at the prison.' This time she did say 'woman'.

'She's black, Mama, but why should that—'

'That's okay then.'

Flo's mother was the only black person to thank me for the video. She wrote that I seemed capable of looking away from my pain and towards the pain of others.

'What do you want me to say to your daughter?' I asked when I told her I had arranged the visit. 'Just visit her,' she replied.

So, there I was, sitting on a tenuous plastic chair in a cold room, *just visiting her*. I looked at my watch; it was eight minutes past three. Through the window in the door, I could see people shuffling past. Probably other prisoners meeting visitors. It's good that they got visitors. I imagined if I were a prisoner, I'd want to get lots of visitors, people who cared about me or brought me news of the outside world. I looked over at the empty chair. For a fleeting moment, it felt like I was the prisoner waiting for a visitor. The thought gave me cold shivers.

When I made the arrangements for the visit, I was told that I'd only have twenty minutes with Flo, that I'd have to leave by twenty-past three. Would these past eight minutes come out of my twenty? I couldn't stay too long beyond twenty-past three anyway; I needed to get back to work. I'd been in this job for six months and didn't want to mess it up. My job title was data capturer, and my boss emphasized that I was a valuable part of the team, even though I knew I could easily be replaced by a cheap machine. I liked the job. I didn't get to see anyone's pain.

I can still see myself sitting in that cold visitors' room, listening to the shuffling outside the door and watching as the door finally opened. Still seated, I turned to the door as a large woman in blue overalls entered. She was followed by an even larger woman in a guard's uniform. The prisoner had chains around her wrists and ankles. The ankle and wrist chains were connected by another chain. Neither of the women looked at me. The guard ushered the prisoner to the plastic chair opposite me, her chains clinking as she shuffled along. 'I'll be right outside,' the guard said as she left. 'Thank you,' I said with a gasp. What I really wanted to say was 'please don't leave'. I watched as the guard took up her position outside the door. I could see her. She looked back into the room, gave me a reassuring nod.

Flo's size surprised me. I imagined seeing a petite teenager, but she looked like a wrestler. Her one-piece blue overalls were tight across her chest and middle. The legs of the uniform ended well above her ankles. She wore grey fabric shoes without socks.

'Hi, my name is Nelson,' I started.

'I'm Flo,' she said. Her tiny voice didn't match her body. I sensed the teenage girl that I expected lurking beneath the massive frame. She spoke softly, sweetly, as we started chatting. I told her that her mother asked me to visit her. She smiled.

'Does sir know my mama?'

'No, I don't know her. I haven't even met her.'

She didn't enquire further. We sat in silence for a moment. I was conscious of our time running out but didn't want her to see me looking at my watch. There really should be a clock in these rooms, I thought to myself.

She leaned forward with her elbows on her knees, slumped her head into her hands. Her untidy braids poured forward like a black waterfall.

'I killed a man,' she finally said. The words filled the room, rose to the ceiling and just hung there. The braids on her head suddenly looked too heavy, like they were pulling on her scalp, threatening to rip off her head. I didn't know what to say, so I said nothing. I felt like hugging her, but I didn't.

She lifted her head to look at me. I could see her anguished face that looked like demons had sunk their claws into her cheeks. I imagined that the oversized bags beneath her eyes held her sins; her sad eyes looked as though they once knew how to smile. I stiffened and reminded myself that I was sitting face to face with a killer, someone who had taken a life. She didn't look like a murderer, but what face does a murderer wear?

She glanced at the door. I looked as well. The guard was still there.

'Are you afraid of what lies ahead?' I asked.

'No, sir, it is the path I must walk. Someone has to die for our sins.'

'Someone has to die for our sins.' I repeated her words.

'I stabbed him in the neck.' Her spirit seemed to recoil as she puked the words. She looked shocked, as though she'd spoken these words for the first time.

'I reported it every time,' she said.

'Reported what?' I said.

'Every time I was raped!'

I gasped.

'Everyone knows,' she continued, with a sadness that made my heart ache. I have known pain but never pain like hers.

'It happens to all the girls in the township. Even if we report it, even if we scream, no one helps. You didn't help. When it happened the fourth time, I killed him. I killed the man who did it.'

I shook my head and blinked my eyes, trying to get some clarity, trying to come to terms with what I'd just heard. 'The fourth time? You were raped four times?' I belted out. She nodded and returned her head to her hands, elbows on her knees, a monument to pain—pain that cannot be soothed.

I wished Mama were there to meet this woman who had done wrong, and not because she was evil. To see that she was not crooked but cracked. To see that those we see as devils are really just injured angels, something inside them bruised or battered or broken. I imagined recording a new video to let the world know that people like Flo are not evil but perhaps are guilty of bearing the sins of our time.

Tears formed in my eyes. I leaned forward again.

'What did you mean "someone has to die for our sins?"' I asked, trying to process it all.

'I know I did wrong, sir,' she stuttered. 'I know I broke commandments.' She slowly raised a sleeve of her blue overalls to wipe across her right eye and cheek, then repeated the motion on the other side. Interesting that she mentioned commandments; Mama made the same reference.

'But you, sir, broke promises.' She looked directly at me and held my gaze.

'Me?' I gawked. 'What promises did I break?'

I leaned back in my chair, feeling confused, accused, attacked. I felt a little anger well up inside. I felt for the pen in my pocket, my weapon of defence in case I needed one. What did she mean I broke promises? What did I have to do with her crime? How dare she—? Before I could finish my thought, she spoke again.

'You didn't help,' she repeated. This was not the inner teenager speaking. This was the outer monster, and she terrified me.

'But I didn't know. How could I have helped? I wasn't there.'

'Would you have helped if you were there?'

That question felt like a hammer to my chest. I began feeling uncomfortable being there with her. The room felt a little smaller. 'Surely my time is up. Where's the guard?' I thought to myself.

I looked at her. She had her eyes fixed on me; her stare felt like fingers prodding me in the chest, insisting on an answer. Would I have helped? Of course, I would have. No, that would be foolish, as Mama would say. I wasn't sure. It would depend. What danger would I be in if I helped? Was the attacker armed? A gangster perhaps, did he have cronies with him? 'It all depends,' I thought to myself. I didn't know, so I didn't answer.

I refocused on Flo. Her blue overalls had faded into the once-blue wall, and all I could see was a black cloud. A few braids were hanging down her face. They looked like the bars of a prison cell, and at that moment I felt unsure about who the prisoner was. She looked at me intently. Her eyes were saying, 'See, you wouldn't have helped.' And she was right.

She got up from her chair. I felt for the pen in my pants pocket again, nudging it so that the end could be easily grabbed. She took her chair, walked towards me, and put it down next to mine. I glanced at the door, through the window. No guard. The guard was gone. It was like a hammer to my forehead this time. As she sat down, I felt hundreds of cockroaches hurrying all over my body, pricking my skin with their needle-like feet.

We were sitting like passengers on a bus, both looking at the wall ahead. I stared at the large grey patches of exposed cement where paint once was, at the pale blue remnants of paint. It looked like a sky, a faint sky with grey clouds, dark grey clouds. I could feel the heaviness of the clouds, the cloud next to me, the approaching winter.

'Someone has to die for our sins,' she growled.

'But—'

'Why did you come here?'

'Your mama—'

'I have no mama.'

'But I got a—'

'I have access to YouTube and Facebook here, you know.' She held out a cell phone as proof.

My head began to spin.

'Why did you come here?' she repeated.

'I came to show you friendship,' I mumbled.

'You're a man; you came here out of guilt.' There was menace in her voice.

I felt sweat forming on my forehead, around my neck, on my back. She blocked my view of the door, so I couldn't see if the guard had returned. I started to get up, but she held me by my forearm and thrust me back down. I felt the plastic chair strain under the force, and for a second, I was more afraid of the chair than of her. She turned her face toward me and repeated, 'Someone has to die for our sins.' The emphasis on *someone* was chilling. My heart sank. I got the message: someone was going to die for our sins, and it wasn't her. The muscles across my body tensed. She tightened her grip on my forearm.

Surely my time was up. Surely the guard was back by now. I wanted to call for help but was too afraid. I was even too afraid to grab my pen. I heard a growing rumble in the corridor. The vibrations on the floor grew stronger. Eventually, I heard screaming and banging as a mass of people raced past the door in the direction of the exit.

'Take off your clothes,' she barked.

'What?'

She was standing in front of me. 'Take off your clothes.'

'Please don't kill me,' I whimpered, the words just fell out of my mouth.

'I'm not going to kill you,' the monster said. 'Others will.'

'What others?'

'You'll see. Just take off your clothes, now!'

I glanced back at the door. No guard, just a blur of people. I removed my jacket, and as my shaking fingers started unbuttoning my shirt, she dropped her chains which appeared to have been loose all along. She started undressing too. She had the top half of her overalls around her waist. She wasn't wearing a bra, revealing the tattoos across her breasts. She took my 3XL shirt which fitted her. She took everything: my denim jacket, woollen scarf, cap, brown pants (with my pen), socks, shoes, even my watch. I kept my underpants and glasses. She bundled her braids into a ball and pressed my cap onto her head. She tossed her overalls and shoes at me. I got into the overalls but left the shoes aside. She threw on my jacket and wrapped my scarf around her neck and face. She noticed me eyeing the heap of chains on the floor.

'Don't do anything foolish,' she said.

'Too late,' I thought to myself, 'I'm here, am I not?'

The door opened, and in a flash, she was gone, part of the stampeding mass.

I scampered over to the corner and sat on the floor, out of sight of those rushing past the room. The prisoners would eventually find me there, a man in a women's prison. As I sat shaking in the corner, the thought that I would not make it back to work in time flitted across my mind.

Three weeks have passed.

I don't remember the gang of prisoners using me as a punching bag and piñata in that prison room. Doctors say I will recover, that I will be able to walk again. The police don't seem to believe that I wasn't an accomplice in Flo's escape. They look at me in disbelief when I talk about my visit as an act of friendship, how I visited her to affirm her humanity.

She still hasn't been found. I sometimes use that word I hate when referring to her. It seems a few people did die that day for her sins and perhaps their own.

As for my sins, well, Mama visits me every day.

She hasn't said it yet, but I know what she's thinking, and when she says it this time, I think I'm likely to agree with her.

COLLECTOR OF MEMORIES

Joshua Chizoma

Mother made me a collector of memories. She taught me that we carry our histories in sacks tied around our necks, adding to their burdens as years lengthen our lives. Each time she told me about the night she found me, she added to my collection. We'd be in the middle of watching a movie and she'd go, 'Do you know you did not cry the first two weeks I brought you home? I was so scared you were dumb.' Or, 'I can't believe you like custard now. As a baby, you only tolerated pap, hot pap like this that did not even burn your throat.' She'd then launch into a narrative punctuated by laughter, pausing only to confirm some detail from her sisters or to disagree with them over one.

Over the years, I learned that she found me on a new year's eve, right about the time the harmattan cold was just picking up, but not boil-water-even-for-doing-dishes freezing yet. That I was wearing a yellow pinafore, swaddled in a blanket that smelled of talcum powder, and that there'd been two different earrings in my ear lobes. I also learned that she found me in an empty carton—a Cabin Biscuit box, she added later.

She reached into the air to pluck those memories whenever she wanted to throw jabs at me about my skin, or my face, or my penchant for eating Cabin Biscuits. However, the first time we had that heart to heart, it had been because of a fight she had with our neighbour, Regina.

We lived in a compound where the houses were spread so far apart as though to pretend it wasn't a public yard. The two-bedroom bungalows squatted in a semi-circle, huddled together like American football players before take-off. It surprised everyone that the landlord who'd had the good sense to build each bungalow separately, would then do something as foolish as making the toilets, shared one to three bungalows, communal. The toilets were often the cause of quarrels. The fights were about who did not flush the toilets well (and left it for their slaves to flush abi?) or who used only one sachet of detergent to improperly wash the toilet (shey those of us that wash with two sachets na fool we be?) or who lost the shared key and was taking their time replacing it. This last reason was the cause of the fight between Mother and Regina.

Regina's son had lost their own key. They'd asked us for ours and had been sharing it with us before the boy, a whole twelve-year-old dimkpa, lost our own key too. Mother had had to suffer the indignity of asking our other neighbour for their key any time we wanted to use the toilet. That day, she made me practically run from school because she was pressed. When we got home, she was about to grab the key when she remembered that it had still not been replaced. Instead of going to ask our other neighbour for theirs, she headed for Regina's house, her handbag still slung over her shoulder.

Regina's church's house fellowship was in full swing when my mother knocked. The tenants had had meetings about these evening fellowships because the attendees sometimes forgot that Regina's parlour was neither their church auditorium nor soundproof. That day, Regina first sent out her son to tell my mother to come back later. When Mother refused, she came out herself.

She wore the face of someone who was being courteous on the pain of death.

'Ah, neighbour. What is this thing that cannot wait for me to finish listening to God's word?' she asked, retying her wrapper laboriously.

My mother told her she was sorry to interrupt but that she wanted to collect money for the new key.

'Ah, I no get plenty money here. In the evening na me go come find you. Abeg, no vex.'

But Mother insisted. She was firm and malleable at the same time, using the tone she used when telling the obnoxious parents of her pupils that, no, she would not go to their house to conduct lessons for their children, they'd have to come to hers. And it worked, because Regina went in and came out with the money scrunched up in her fist.

Perhaps, it was the way Regina gave her the money, almost throwing it at her, that my mother had had to clap the air to catch the notes. Or maybe it was not really the money that was peppering her, maybe my mother just wanted to be petty, because as she turned to leave, she gave as a parting shot:

'Do I blame you? Is it not because I am sharing a compound with an illiterate like you?'

'Don't even come for me. O gini di? Who does not know children make mistakes?' Regina shouted.

My mother could not have aimed her punch lower. Everyone in the compound knew Regina's story and how she'd clawed her way from poverty.

'If your world is complete, go and fetch water with a basket na. Nonsense and nonsense.'

'It is okay,' her church members said. They were standing on her verandah; an emergency recess had been called, no doubt.

'Leave me. Every time she will be carrying face for somebody like say na she better pass. She thinks we do not know her shameful secret. If I open this my mouth for her eh, she will pack out of this compound.'

When my mother heard this, she dropped her bag and every pretence of civility with it.

'You see that thing you want to say, you must say it today oo.'

She clapped her hands together and came to stand in front of Regina, pushing her breasts onto her face.

'E pass say I pick child for gutter? E pass am? Oya, talk na?'

Regina did not respond. She was probably too shocked to. Even I had not expected the drama to take such a swift turn.

'Good. I think say you no dey fear.' My mother turned around then and saw me. Her face became a mélange of conflicting emotions: anger, shame, remorse. But anger won. She grabbed me and said, 'Who asked you to follow me?' Although she hadn't asked me not to.

That night she bristled with anger, and even grading papers did not help. Eventually, she dropped the pen and called me to her side.

'Chibusonma, come here,' she said.

I walked over from the sofa to the single chair she was sitting on. She shifted and I squeezed in with her. She stroked my arm, and I could feel the flames within her tempering, losing their rage.

Aunty looked up from her phone, and Chidinma paused the movie she was watching, trapping Ramsey Nouah's face on the screen.

'It is better you hear it from my mouth,' she began.

It was one of those things you knew. The way yes was yes and no was no. They were definites, and I could hold them to my breast, my history. That night, my mother did not romanticize the idea that I was an abandoned child she had picked up. She said it in a matter-of-fact way, like she was teaching me to memorize numbers, like she wanted me to know just for the sake of it. As I grew older and recognized that bricks and sticks sometimes are no match for words, I was grateful. Because after that day I realized how things could shape-shift if you had no sight. Snide remarks and snarky jokes found context and became decipherable. But because my mother did not burden my story with the weight of shame, I had none to spare. Even beyond that, I was hemmed in on every side by love, from my mother and her two sisters. Their love cushioned the effect of the taunts from the other children, fashioned me an armour that bricks and sticks and words could not penetrate.

Rhoda, whom everyone called Aunty, was the oldest and had a hairdressing salon. Her sisters did not go to her shop. They said her hands were 'painful', although they made sure it was only the walls of our house that heard them say so. She loved 'living' and was the one who bought the TV and paid for the light bill. Each time the bill came, she'd divide the sum and remind her sisters each morning to contribute, placing her share on the centre table so 'everyone could see she had done her part'. Seven out of ten times she'd eventually go to pay it herself, gaining monopoly over the TV remote and daring anyone to change the channel even when she fell asleep watching Super Story.

Chidinma, the middle child, sold recharge cards and phone accessories. She was the most generous of the three, the one with the least savings too. They used to say, 'Except Chidinma does not have, that's why she will not give you. If she has money and you have a need, forget it.'

Mother was a primary four teacher. She taught the class for years, even when she got her teacher's training certificate, even when she got a university degree through distance learning. She refused to leave for another class. Her name was Florence, but most people knew her as 'Aunty Primary Four'.

Mother mothered me exclusively when it came to meting out

punishment. Her sisters would tally all my infractions, waiting for her return so they'd bear witness. At the end my mother would respond, 'You mean she was this stupid, and you did not beat her?' incredulity lacing her tone, after which she'd drag me close and give me a whooping herself. But apart from this area, the three sisters fed me their different flavours of motherhood. It usually was Aunty who bought me clothes and made my hair every weekend. Saturday evenings she'd bring out the kitchen stool to our corridor, spread her legs, and trap my body within her warmth. Sometimes it was a whole family affair, with Mother shining a torch and Chidinma separating and handing out the attachments. I did not have the luxury of protesting her painful hand. It was enough that I debuted a new hairstyle each Monday morning. Pain was a small price to pay.

Chidinma bought me the UTME form for the polytechnic I ended up going to. I'd written JAMB the first time and failed. When I wrote it for the second time and failed again, Mother did not say anything. I knew she was beginning to think that the first failure was not a fluke. I passed the third time with a small margin, and Chidinma bought me a form for the polytechnic.

That day, she called me to her shop, brought out the papers, and in a voice that entertained no arguments said,

'Fill this thing, my friend.'

I stared at the paper on the table. None of my friends went to the polytechnic. Who would? University students were the *shit*. They returned home only during the holidays, bamboo stalk thin and sporting lingo that included 'projects' and 'lectures' and 'handouts'. They got away with many things, especially those who went to schools with ear-famous names like the University of Ibadan and the University of Nigeria. Plus, everybody and their nannies knew that it was the 'not-so-bright' students who settled for the polytechnic.

I considered my options for a while. They weren't many.

'I am going to live off-campus. I will not be going from the house,' I said.

'Okay,' Chidinma replied. We both understood it was a bargain. That was a compromise she could take to her sisters.

I started dating Chike in my final year, four years ago. He was a customer care agent at a mobile phone company and had once helped me do a SIM card welcome back. Chike was affable and took the job of being a nice person very seriously. He was the kind of person who would never refuse going the extra mile but complained while doing the task. Good-natured complaints about how it was taking his time or how he was tired, in such a way that it was not really grumbling, seeming almost like a normal conversation.

I moved in with him after graduation. By that time, I had spent so many weekends at his place that the one time I did not come home on a Monday, Mother did not bother asking me what happened. It was like a natural occurrence, like night giving birth to day or weeds sprouting in the rainy season. One day I was living with my mother and her two sisters, the next I was going from Chike's house to the bank where I worked.

Every time he mentioned marriage, I packed my bags and went to Binez hotels down the street. The manager knew me and usually assigned me the one room with good netting on the door. Chike always came for me after two days or so; the longest he'd stayed without me was seven days. The last time he came to pick me, he had been dripping with righteous anger and asked me whether it was not time to stop my childishness.

Whenever I think of it, I wonder if I hadn't moved in with Chike, if my attention hadn't been consumed by that puerile drama we were intent on performing, whether the events that followed afterwards would have been different. Whether I would have caught my mother's sickness earlier, or more appropriately, traced its root and found its cure. But like a hen, I took my eyes off Mother for a minute—such that I was unaware of how dire things were at home the Friday Aunty and Chidinma visited me at work—and a kite swooped in.

That day, I was wearing a new Ankara dress. Chidinma sat on a plastic chair in the reception area and Aunty came to stand before me, speaking to me in snatches while I attended to customers. In between clearing withdrawal slips and receiving deposits, Aunty managed to tell me to come by the house in the evening for an urgent matter and I was able to feign that the most pressing thing then was the zip of the new dress cutting into my back, and not the scary reality of what it meant for my aunts to visit me at my place of work to summon me home.

In the evening, I stopped on my way home to buy bananas, then remembering that Mother preferred oranges, I bought those instead. Then, in order not to offend the seller, I decided to pay for both.

The light was on when I stepped into the house. Mother was lying on the couch in the parlour. The room was thick with gloom such that even though the light was on, it was as though the darkness was winning.

'How is she? Is she getting any better?' I asked.

My aunts shook their heads. It was odd how they just sat down doing nothing. I placed the items on the table and sat at the foot of the couch Mother was lying on.

'Chibusonma, your mother has something to tell you.' Aunty's words sliced the silence.

Chidinma went to Mother and helped her up.

Mother stared right ahead, mute.

'You will not tell her now? What is wrong with you?' Chidinma said. 'You don't want what is holding you to leave you eh?'

Mother shuddered, as though the words actually made physical contact with her. I was quiet. The spectacle, it seemed, was for me.

'See, Chibusonma, there are some things I've not told you about the night I found you.' Her voice was low, but I listened nonetheless, my ears sharpening to pick up stray words.

'Yes, it was on a new year's eve, and Pastor Gimba gave a powerful message that day. I was still tingling with the power when I saw you at the dump. Or rather, heard you. That in itself was a miracle given all the New Year bangers going off that night. But it wasn't at Crescent Street. I went to the church at Faulks road. We had a combined service that night.'

'How are any of these important kwanu?' Chidinma interrupted.

'Keep quiet,' Aunty said.

Mother gave a deep sigh.

'Chibusonma, I did not find you. Your mother was around then. I took you from her,' she said.

I stood rock still and let the information wash over me.

'She'd given birth weeks before and did not let anyone touch the baby. She even chased the police away when they came. That night she was so tired. When I came by, I told her I'd hold you small, and she said okay. Then she fell asleep. I took you and left.'

She rushed through the story, barely pausing to take a break, suddenly seeming to be in a hurry. When she was done, she was winded and had to lay back down.

'Why was she at the dump?' I asked.

'Your mother was a madwoman. She was not by the dump, really. She had a small shack that she stayed in.'

'I see,' I said. 'So, you lied to me?'

'Technically, it was not a lie,' Chidinma said.

'All my life I thought that my mother abandoned me. That maybe she was one of those careless girls who threw away their babies. Wait, so you stole me from my mother?' I said.

'I am sorry,' Mother said.

'You erased my mother? What am I supposed to do with this

information now?'

'I'm sorry.'

'Chibusonma. We felt it was for the best,' Aunty said. 'What your mother told you was for the best. Would you have preferred the truth? That a madwoman is your mother?'

'You probably would have died from the cold or caught an infection or something,' Chidinma added.

'You don't know that,' I said.

'You don't know that too,' she returned.

I felt ganged up on. And then my mother said again, 'I am sorry.'

'Why are you telling me this now?' I asked.

There was a shift in the mood. It was as though the sisters were waiting for something else.

'Before I took you.' She paused and a film of terror slipped into her eyes. 'Your mother said that if I didn't hand you back that I will always know no peace.' She looked away. It was the end.

Aunty took over.

'Ever since my sister became sick, I told her this thing was spiritual, but she did not listen. Now, after three tests, nothing nothing,' she said.

'Look at her. She has been like this since morning. But thank God for Pastor Gimba. He got a revelation from God that your mother offended someone, and she needs to make peace,' Aunty continued.

'How?' I asked.

Chidinma brought out a folder and handed it to me. Their actions were like a well-rehearsed choreography, like actors on a stage acting out a script. I flipped through the content.

'We've managed to trace your birth mother. Her family house is in Nkwerre. They came and carried her from the dump after a while. We believe she is the one your mother has to make peace with,' Chidinma said.

That night, after I came back from Mother's, I cried when Chike spanked me. He became even more scared when I asked him to make love to me gently. He was fidgeting as though it was our first time. Eventually, I had to climb on top, controlling the rhythm of the thrusts myself.

I woke up the next morning to the sight of him holding a tray and wearing a nervous smile. I sat up and held out my hand for the tray. He'd made pap and fried plantains.

'Sorry, I could not go to buy eggs,' he said.

'No problems,' I said, biting into the plantains. They were well done, and I was surprised.

'So, about yesterday, what happened?' He came to sit beside me. He didn't know what to do with his hands. He kept them on the bed for a while, then touched his collar.

'Just go.'

'Why? You don't want to talk to me?'

'Just go abeg. I'm not in the mood,' I said.

He got up, smoothened his shirt, and left.

On our way to Nkwerre, Chidinma got into an argument with the driver. She thought he was driving too fast, to which he'd replied that she had no business telling him how to drive his own car. I wanted to reach out to smack Chidinma. I did not understand how she had space in her head to notice other things, like how the seats were cramped—she complained about that—or that I used makeup—she didn't think that was appropriate. And how could she have a problem with the driver's speed? Wasn't speed important to us?

When I asked them that morning how they knew the particular place we were going, Aunty said, 'We've been planning this thing for a while now, Chibusonma. Let's just go.'

'How about my mother, is she not coming with us?' I craved a fight, an outlet for the nameless emotions broiling within me.

'No,' Chidinma said.

'We will still go again,' Aunty added, a little cheerily. 'That time, we will go with a lot more of our people.'

Chidinma came to me and took my two hands in hers. Her eyes held such kindness and love that I felt my rage buckle.

'Nne, I know that you are angry, and you should be. But can you postpone your anger one more day? Just after today you can be angry all you want. Can you do that?'

At Ngor Okpala, Aunty bought me a packet of plantain chips, handed me a handkerchief when I started sobbing, and placed my head on her shoulder. No words were exchanged.

The house we went to had a huge bird on the gate. The bird split into two when the gate was opened. The inside of the compound was swept clean. The patterns the broom made on the ground was beautiful. It had rained the night before, so the ground still retained enough moisture to make sweeping less arduous and more like a process in making art.

A group of people sat on the verandah—men and women whose generations were far removed from mine. A man broke away and went straight for Aunty.

'You must be Rhoda,' he said in perfectly enunciated English. 'My name is Peter. I am the person you have been communicating with.'

Aunty bowed a little.

'Is she our daughter?' He asked. Aunty nodded, smiling broadly to emphasize the good news.

'Oh, welcome, our daughter.'

He came and gave me a swift embrace. Several women came out to hug me, as though I'd been declared safe for communal interaction. They held me with an air of familiarity that surprised me. I was led to a seat. They sat around me, smiling and asking questions I didn't have to think about before I answered: what school I went to, whether I was married, if I knew I had my biological mother's nose.

A hush descended when one woman came out from the backyard. Her hair was shaved to a crop and she wore a gown that hung off her shoulder, revealing the strap of a black bra. She had on a static smile, not widening into laughter or extinguishing into a frown.

She came and pulled me up and hugged me. When I looked up, I noticed that more than one woman had tears in their eyes. The woman walked with me back the way she came.

At the backyard, she brought two seats and placed them side by side. She told me that she sold tomatoes at the market and lived here with her brother's family. She was a member of the Legion of Mary and loved going for the Latin mass. She shaved all of her hair because relaxers made her scalp itch, but she wore wigs when she went to church.

She talked and I listened, noting that her life revolved around the church, maybe a little too much, and that she did not ask me anything about myself, this woman that was my birth mother. Some of the women sat nearby, listening too as though they were not familiar with the details she was sharing.

'I know what you are thinking, but I am fine now. I take my medications dutifully, and I go for my doctor's appointment whenever I have to,' she said after a while.

I reached out and flicked lint from her gown.

'It is manageable. Not everyone dies from dementia. That is what my doctor says I should call it, dementia.' She laughed. The women shifted uncomfortably in their seats.

'My mother—'

I began and then paused. I had not considered that there would be a need to call my real mother anything other than Mother. The woman did not respond. I continued,

'My mother tells me you said something to her the night she took me from you. She said you told her something dangerous would happen to her if she took me.'

Her face remained free of ripples. She still looked up at me as though expecting me to add something.

'I want to know what it is. I want you to forgive her.'

'I can't remember. Is she sure?' she asked.

'Yes, she is.'

'I can't remember. Things upstairs are jumbled up.' For a moment, the smile slipped, and I saw something that looked like fear lurking beneath the mask.

'Okay. But I think you should maybe forgive her.'

'Okay, I do.'

I sighed, exasperated.

'Maybe you should do something, like a ritual?'

'I don't know,' she said. 'Oya why don't you kneel down and let me pray for you,' she said.

I kneeled. She placed her hands on my head.

'May the curse pass over you. I forgive your mother.'

When I lifted my eyes, she was smiling. It was the same smile she had on before. It seemed like mockery now. Aunty quickly looked away when I stood up. But in her eyes, I'd seen prayers.

That evening, a petulant expression sat on Chike's face when he came in. He walked around, his displeasure as imposing as a billboard, but I ignored him. Finally, when we were in bed, he asked, 'Where did you go today?'

'Somewhere,' I replied.

He sighed.

'My people have found a woman for me. Since you are not ready,' he said.

Even though I'd noticed the steady exodus of his clothes from the closet, it still stung to hear him say it out loud. I was briefly scared. What if he left and I discovered that I actually loved him? What if I told him I was ready to marry him now?

'I hope she knows that you like getting pegged?' I said instead.

'I don't like getting pegged,' he said.

'And all these sex toys, better carry them with you.'

He said nothing.

'Your new bride, you think she'll like being tied up, or she'll rim you well? It did take me a while to learn how to do it.'

'Just stop.'

'Plain vanilla sex, imagine how you'll miss me pegging you.'

I started laughing. He swung over and climbed on top of me. He placed his hands around my windpipe.

'I don't like getting pegged. If you tell people that nonsense about me, I will kill you,' he snarled.

Around midnight, when my phone started ringing, it caught me awake. By then, I was busy rearranging the contents of my sack of memories, deciding the ones that would stay and the ones that would go. It was futile. Even though my mother's betrayal ran deep, I knew which version of that night I was going to hold on to.

'Answer the call na or turn the phone off,' Chike grumbled and then grabbed the phone and said, 'Aunty.'

The ringing stopped, his hands still stretched out to me. It started again, and Chike placed the phone on the bed.

'Are you really going to leave me? Did they really find you another woman?' I asked.

'Jesus! What is this? What is going on?' Chike said, alarm stark in his eyes.

I did not respond. Instead, clouds gathered and a noisy deluge fell from the sky of my eyes. Frustration and anger flowed downwards, accompanied by an unlearned dirge I didn't know I could manage. My voice grew hoarse, and Chike left the room, but the phone wouldn't stop ringing. Aunty called, Chidinma called, and I let them. My tears were helplessness made flesh, an attempt to stretch time's finiteness and leave unchecked possibilities. Because I knew that on the other side of that phone was maybe a prayer unanswered.

ETHIO-CUBANO
Desta Haile

ኢትዮጵያ ታበፀዕ እደዋሃ ሃበ እግዚአብሐር
Ethiopia shall soon stretch out her hands unto God.
(Psalm 68:31)

¡Patria o Muerte!
(Fidel Castro)

Havana 2015

'Ay, Eleggua!'

The old woman chuckled and set the wooden statue upright again. 'Why are you always causing trouble?' she asked it affectionately. She smiled as if she heard a response that we couldn't. The collection of sticks looked slick with viscous liquid, feathers, beads, and cowrie shells sprinkled around it. It could have been my imagination overheating after hours of traipsing through la Habana Vieja in the midday sun, but the inanimate structure actually seemed to be breathing. Casual. My eyes widened.

When she closed the door, it was clear we had stepped into another world. Two turtles crept through the cool, high-ceilinged space. Another one, weary of the visitors, peered out from a magenta plastic bowl full of water. Elephant-ear plants jostled for space to dance amongst carved wooden furniture and lace curtains, dripping ivory candles and sumptuous paintings. The old woman greeted us, motioned for us to sit down, and chided my friend for bringing me along to the *misa*, as our spirits might get confused and jumbled up when trying to communicate. 'How will I know who is who?' she complained. The colourful bird in the elaborate wrought-iron cage trilled, concording. I looked down sheepishly at the thyme-coloured tiles.

Religious figures adorned the walls, a freestyle amalgamation of orishas and Catholic saints, deft and flexible disguises to protect the African gods. Eleggua, Saint Anthony. Chango became Saint Barbara. Oshun, Our Lady of Charity. Mariam.

Brussels 2003

Teferi's clandestine restaurant was packed as usual, his living room welcoming a handful of Habesha hungry for tastes of home. The television spun a rotation of Ethiopian hits as Teferi carried on conversations from his tiny but miraculous kitchen. The strains of Aster Aweke and Mahmoud Ahmed floated over the chatter and mingled with the tantalising aromas drifting from the simmering *wot*, as Haile Selassie gazed sternly over the scene from his silver frame on the wall.

Sipping sweet spiced tea as we waited for our meal, one of the guests got a phone call, and an unexpected clatter of fluent Spanish met the person at the other end of the line. I was surprised as Teferi's place was generally an exclusively Habesha hub, and this guy looked pretty recognizably so with his almond eyes, reddish-brown complexion, and generous forehead. When he put his phone down, I asked him where he was from. 'I'm Ethio-Cubano,' he said curtly.

At a party weeks later, I spotted the same guy—gold chain, belt printed with most, if not all, of the flags of the world—serving salsa steps like no other Habesha I've ever seen. Habesha guys got the shoulders on lock, but Cubans got the hips. Picking up on the stilted conversation from Chez Teferi, we started talking, and I asked whether he'd grown up in Ethiopia or Cuba. 'Ethiopia,' he said, 'until they sent us to Cuba.'

'Sent you?' I asked. 'How do you mean?' He smirked and shimmied away, disappearing into the dance. As I was leaving, walking down the narrow staircase, I felt a sloppy *beso* splat on my neck and turned in shock to see the inebriated mystery man. I dashed for the front door and into my waiting cab, breathing a sigh of relief.

New York 2015

I sat on the sofa in the cramped Spanish Harlem apartment as the lady murmured to my friend in Spanglish. Her hands fluttered over the cards she had laid out on the table, and she presented *mi amiga* with spiritual routes out of her predicament. Clear glasses of varying sizes, full of water, dotted her kitchen counter, with tiny bubbles sparkling on each surface. 'It means they are happy,' she had explained earlier. Lighting tall botanica candles, she sprinkled Agua de Florida liberally.

'Honey, you want a reading too?'

'Me? Oh, I uh, nah, it's okay.'

'Venga, siéntate.'

So I sat before her, and she lit a cigarette and reshuffled, recentred. A crescent of cards cut out before me; she translated each one. Travels, spirits, water. 'All the travelling is good, you know; some of those negative spirits, they don't like crossing water like that; you can shake them off. Going back and forth over the ocean *así*, it can help.' She froze.

'Mami, are you African?'

'Yes?'

'Because there's a lady here . . . she's all in white. Wearing sandals.' She was trembling slightly. 'She's got some kinda tattoo on her neck? A cross?' she whispered in Nuyorican. She kept glancing to her right, to her invisible interlocutor. She closed her eyes and bowed her head. Concentrating, tense, she shook.

'She keeps saying something. I don't understand. It's in some African language. Something "dough," something "dough?" She keeps ending sentences with "dough?"'

She slumped, and her breathing was scratchy.

'Oye, one of you got to go get me some Nat Shermans. Menthol. *Por fa*.' She shuddered. I raced out the door, propelled by the realization that this Cuban lady had just had a one-sided conversation with my Tigrinya-speaking grandmother from some frequency beyond. The question suffix in Tigrinya, the 'dough' that she was hearing, sounds just like that: ዶ. '*Gracias mi vida*,' she thanked me as I handed the packet to her when I got back what seemed like seconds later.

A solo trip to the corner store late at night in a city I barely knew had suddenly struck me as not a great idea, and I had sped up, lamenting the fact I couldn't go faster. If my grandmother could transmit messages directly from the Akeleguzay afterlife, then surely I should be able to teleport to and from the neighbourhood bodega? How was it that despite this victory of intercultural, interdimensional mediumship, a language barrier was still lodged firmly in place? I was confused. This world makes no sense. None of these worlds makes any sense.

London 2017

The play featured actors who were survivors of torture, trafficking, or both. Multilingual refugee men and women who had fallen between the cracks in their countries, documents, dictators. These brave souls were standing on stage, now safe, far away from their oppressors, reclaiming their dignity and autonomy through creativity and speech.

One actor. I just knew. His Ethiopian features combined with the Cuban lilt in his voice, the loose conclusions of his sentences. 'Are you Ethio-Cubano?' I asked him in the foyer after the performance. He was startled. He grabbed my hand. 'How did you know?'

Sipping expensive and tasteless mojitos near London Bridge months later, I realized hardly any combination of cultures could be as evasive and cagey as Ethiopian and Cuban. My attempt at finding out more about this seemingly secret chapter in history was inconclusive and vague, and my interviewee became increasingly fresh.

Washington D.C 1981
CIA Report

> *Fidel Castro's decision to intervene militarily in Ethiopia was largely at Moscow's behest and reflected a convergence of Cuban and Soviet interests. Havana and Moscow view Chairman Mengistu Hailemariam as a revolutionary trying to transform Ethiopian society. Moscow, in particular, prized Ethiopia as the major power in a strategic region.*
>
> *Cuban combat troops in Ethiopia suffer from serious morale problems because of homesickness, limited pay and lack of leave. Many are reservists and most are in their late-teens and early twenties. They are bored and prone to misconduct and drunkenness. Some have apparently sold goods on the black market to get money to buy narcotics. The Cubans have had some problems in getting food to their liking. Occasional failures in getting food to the troops on a timely basis have forced them to steal from the local population.*
>
> *The Ethiopians who come in contact with the Cubans*

seem to prefer them to the cliquish and arrogant Soviets. The Cubans are more inclined than the Soviets to generate goodwill by learning the local language and customs. The most serious problems between Ethiopian civilians and the Cubans—incidents often involving women and drinking—occur around major military garrisons such as Dire Dawa.

The Internet 2007

Dear Ethio-Cuban community,

I am writing this notice statement to address some issues that have been brought to my attention in regards to the production of the documentary 'The Unhealing Wound'. Before I begin, I would like to offer my sincere apology and also heartfelt gratitude for those Ethio-Cubans who were courageous enough to tell their story. None of us had foreseen that this much criticism and hardship would fall on those participants. It is quite disturbing and saddening that those interviewed have been shunned from the larger community for sharing their story in the spirit of preserving their own personal history and lives . . .

(Open letter from Aida Muluneh to the Ethio-Cuban community)

Havana 2016

The waves rushed up to reach us as we sat on the Malecón, dangling our legs and nursing our Cuba Libres in their plastic cups. The sky was purple-black with blinding white stars pressed into it.

He was expanding on the pantheon of Orishas that ruled over every element of existence. He scrutinized me. 'You have to go to a babalawo, do a whole ceremony to find out who your Orisha parents really are. Yours could be Oshun, maybe. Or Yemaya. Yemaya rules the sea. But just the living part. The bottom of the sea is the kingdom of Olokun. Olokun is less known, not really male or female, just is. My dad's Orisha is Olokun. He's real quiet, you know, but strong. Some say if a baby is born with their umbilical cord wrapped around their neck, their destiny lies with Olokun.'

'Who is your Orisha?' I asked.

'Ogun,' he said, tugging his green and black bead necklace out of his shirt. 'Can't you see I'm a warrior?'

'You're goofy,' I pointed out.

He broke into a laugh and showed mock offence. 'Ogun is the Orisha of iron. If he's angry at people, he ends them with something like a car accident, something messy and metallic like that.'

A building that resembled an upright coffin loomed over us with each floor radiating different colour lighting: azure, faded gold, bronze, azure, faded gold. The Wi-Fi 'zombies' clustered around a nearby fountain, gazing hypnotized at their screens, praying the precarious connection would hold up.

Days later, we walked along a deserted beach of Habana del Este while the winds stirred up the water, the sky muting into grayscale menace. The palm trees, like so many ballerinas with their arms in fourth position, practising plié, cambré, the fronds pirouetting through the gathering zephyr. He recalled being so hungry while doing obligatory military service that he would climb to the top of the palms to try and dislodge the coconuts, and once, losing his grip, he slid all the way down and shredded his skin.

A potpourri of animal bones littered the little gutters we were hurriedly stepping over, remnants of rituals and offerings. 'Sometimes the sewage system of Havana gets clogged up,' he said, shaking his head, 'with the detritus of the ceremonies. The amount of action in Cayo Hueso, alone!'

Back at the house, the gale battered the roof, making the windows creak and groan. I rustled in my bag for my frankincense, my Eritrean Express (never leave home without it). I heated charcoal over the stove and gingerly placed lumps of the milky resin on the glowing heat. The smoke rose quickly, perfuming the house and calming me instantly. *'Eres santera?'* he asked me, eyes lit with surprise and curiosity. I cracked up. 'I'm no santera. I'm Solomonic,' I joked. A song came to my mind's eye as the soothing smoke swirled, comforting every corner.

> *Santa Maria del Mar, man, he Cuban*
> *All good so far and we groovin'*
> *Santero, but that's alright yeah 'cause*
> *He kinda Habesha when he all in white*
> *Got married at 3 a.m.*
> *Obrapia rooftop, all wrapped in love*
> *Made me a palm-frond ring, where you come from king*
> *Make me want to sing: Hosanna!*

Addis Abeba 1976

Reesom, the journalist, had a sweaty grip on his camera. His nerves were mounting. He and his colleague, Tabotu, had left the rally for Mengistu, and there was palpable fear back at the radio station. 'We need to leave,' he told Tabotu. 'And quickly. It's too dangerous. They'll come for us next.'

Later that week he got into a crunching car accident that flipped the car and delivered him an excruciating blow to the spine. Mother Mariam must have been watching over him at the moment of impact because he managed to crawl out of the upturned vehicle alive, inching his way to the side of the road where he collapsed. The beeps, traffic, exhaust fumes, lights, shouts, and cries of the drivers and passers-by formed a chaotic constellation over Reesom's agonized body. An old, leathery face loomed over him and exclaimed: *'Ooway!* Are you okay? Thank God, my son, thank God! You almost needed one of these!' He gestured to the pyramid of simple wooden coffins he was selling at the side of the road. 'Praise

God! Today is your second birthday. Praise God! Praise Mariam!'

Reesom had a nightmare later, of standing on a bridge and looking down at the water, illuminated by a surreal glow that was darkened and drowned in a vermilion tide. Mengistu soon made a dramatic speech with three bottles full of what looked like blood, forcefully throwing them one by one, each shattering and spilling on the ground. *Crash! Crash! Crash!*

Brussels 2001

El Goyo stood by the studio's open door, drawing long and thoughtful puffs of his cigarette. The clouds he exhaled met the chill air and the stinging, relentless silver pellets of rain pinging from the sky. The dancers panted, struggling to catch their breath, stretching their muscles and wiping beads of perspiration from their faces. Goyo pivoted sharply and walked back into the room, his back extraordinarily straight. He clapped his hands, sending the sound ricocheting around the room, alerting everyone to prepare for the drums and the drums to prepare for everyone. Each drum is a trinity of living things; one: the skin stretched over, two: the wood, and three: the impulse of the drummers' beat. El Goyo's sinuous and sculpted ebony frame commands the rhythm, tells the stories, beckons the spirits. He calls us all back into position.

Ochosi!
Ode mata oré oré
Ochosi!
Ode mata oré oré

Havana 2017

'Did you just put salt on the pineapple? That's nasty. Why on earth would you do that?'

'Try it,' he grinned, 'it brings the taste out.'

We had very different definitions of taste. All we could agree on was coffee. Leaving breakfast and walking down to the shore, we passed a family I was almost certain was Ethiopian. I stared at them not sure, they stared at me not sure, and the moment passed as he, oblivious, put his arm around me and said something or other I didn't hear, zoned out. I looked back to see but the moment had evaporated, it was too late to go back.

Isla de la Juventud 2020

> *Today we celebrate the 40th anniversary of the arrival of the second contingent of martyrs' children, the children of those who fell in the battles of Ogaden in the East and Eritrea in the North, invited to Cuba to study for free, generously provided for by Fidel Castro for his comrade Mengistu Hailemariam. Twenty-two days of travel on the Soviet ship Leonid Sobinov, from the 11th of November to the 2nd of December. Through their studies and development as Communists, the children continue the heroic service to their country.*

The Ethiopian orphans, who had arrived after three weeks of open sea, were welcomed to what was to be their new home. La Evangelista. Isla de Cotorras. Isla de Tesoros. The island had had many names. Likewise, many of the children would adopt new names. That is until they were eighteen and strong enough, in their communist education and ideals, to return to the motherland and help construct its future. At least, that was the plan.

Amharic was traded for Spanish, injera for *ropa vieja*, and the boarding schools grew amongst the citrus groves to house thousands of them, some 12,000 kilometres from home. Eventually, numerous young Namibians and Angolans would become their neighbours, more young communists to be trained for Africa. The largest building on the island was the panopticon Model Prison that had once housed the Castro brothers. If you squinted your eyes enough, the brutal circular buildings resembled rolls of injera, with its multitude of tiny windows representing the bread's 'thousand eyes'.

Asmara 1955

Herding the animals, young Reesom stepped on a thorn. He cried out and winced, but it was impossible to pluck it out and any effort just drove it deeper into the sole. He dared not tell his mother about it because she was quick to cut. Well-practised, she made incisions with jagged broken glass to cure swollen glands or any other afflictions poor family members might have. She took to it with the confidence of a medical doctor, not like a woman who never had the chance to go to school. He did not want to risk it.

He put a brave face on and kept schtum. Eventually, the dull pain subsided. It wasn't until decades later, somewhere in the Caribbean, on assignment with the UN, that a sharp twinge sent aches shooting right up his leg until he asked reception to call him a doctor. He described the pain, in stilted Spanish, to the doctor, a Cuban, who listened as he examined him. The doctor spied a small dark line poised just under the skin of Reesom's foot. He deftly removed it with local anaesthetic, returning the errant acacia thorn to the shepherd boy who had stepped on it many moons ago. Reesom was stunned. He fell into a feverish sleep with this vicious antique on his night table and limped through his dreams.

Havana 2014

We landed on July 26th to much fanfare and giant flags cascading down the buildings, rippling large in black and red. 'Is this for us?' I asked my travel companion, bemused. 'No, you fool,' she quipped. 'It's for the 26th of July Movement. The revolution. Read a book!'

I arrived in la Habana for the first time with a crown of full albaso. The rhino ridges of the traditional Habesha hairstyle made me feel regal at the family reunion and festivities over the weekend in Minnesota, but now in the humid Cuban sun, I was itching to remove it. The strategically-placed yarn and elaborate extensions worked in Abyssinian highland weather but were not designed for neotropical settings.

The Chinese lantern trees lined the coastal drive, blood-red rubies nestled in the leaves. We took a 16-hour bus ride down to Santiago de Cuba. It had been impossible to ascertain exact dates of the carnival there, but having been convinced by a Cuban friend it was worth the trip, we arrived at what appeared to be a morning-after-the-party scene. The streets were empty; stray dogs strolled as everyone recovered indoors from the festivities we had just missed. We hitched a ride back to Havana with people who stopped at houses in almost every province, knocking on doors to illicitly stock up on the dairy products that were impossible to find in the capital.

London 1998

'You know, my poetry, I want it to be sung.' Reesom confided, while pushing the black beans and rice around his plate. He always dissed the monotony of Cuban food but nonetheless insisted on returning to the same little Cuban joint off High Street Kensington with its checkered tablecloths and violent coffee.

'I want my poem to be to Eritrea what "Guantanamera" is to Cuba,' he continued. 'But without any communist strings attached. All these systems,' he sighed. 'Let the truth be the system. You know that Mengistu Hailemariam is still alive, he lives in Harare?'

'Harar, Ethiopia?'

'No, Harare, Zimbabwe. Special guest of Mugabe.' He finished the last morsel of plantain and wiped his mouth with his napkin. 'This great musician, Melake Ghebre, from Walias Band, this Ethiopian group from the seventies, who went on tour to the States with Mahmoud Ahmed and never returned . . . these, these exiles who settled on the East Coast,' he explained. 'Melake said something I've never forgotten: "Doctors treat patients, but musicians treat the country."' *'Elelelelelelelele! Ezm! Be-ebm! Ezm!'* he ululated and laughed, shrugging his shoulders to an impromptu Habesha boogie breakdown, and then put his hand up for the check.

Moscow 2009

We snuck out of Hotel Cosmos in the north of the city to do some quick and ill-advised sightseeing. Racist attacks in Moscow had been all too frequent in the previous six months, and we had been warned to be very, very careful.

We still managed to explore a bit, two African women on a tourist mission. Red Square with its multicoloured onion domes. A cathedral where beautiful, haunting music was sung and Russian Orthodox Jesus peered out of each painting looking vexed. We got lost trying to find Chekhov's House. Finally, we made it to the Pushkin Museum where an argument was settled.

'Aha! There. You see. I told you. Pushkin is Habesha. Done.' I beamed triumphantly to my sceptical friend. I pointed to the tiny grey plaque stuck unceremoniously to the wall of the Pushkin museum, explaining the genealogy that linked their national treasure of a writer to Abram Petrovich Hannibal. 'Abyssinia, baby. So you can tell that to Cameroon and Chad. Russia's literary prince is Habesha.'

My friend shook her head. 'You guys, always trying to claim everybody.'

'Lies!' I protested.

London 2019

Soon after the plane took off, I felt I was being watched. Intensely. I glanced up and indeed I was. Smushed between the airplane seat and the window was a chubby, cherubic little face, her big brown eyes intently fixed on me.

'What's your name?' she asked.

'My name is Desta. What's yours?'

'Dahlia,' she giggled, cheeks dimpling.

'Nice to meet you, Dahlia.'

She giggled again and decided that we were friends. Best friends. She turned around and clambered up onto her seat, inquisitive at first, then bolder, offering me her peanuts, then outright squealing and jiggling as she reached over to squeeze my face and clutch at my curls: 'I have hair like you,' she declared. The stewardesses *awwwed* at our spontaneous and passionate friendship.

Her dad smiled apologetically over his shoulder and told her to sit down properly, gently scolding her back into her seatbelt in Spanish. She soon turned around to me again, peering between the seat and the window. 'I'm bored,' she whined.

'Only boring people get bored is what my dad used to tell me when I was your age,' I offered. 'I'm not boring!' she bellowed, much to my amusement and embarrassment. To be fair, I would retort the same way whenever my dad said it.

'*Mi amor*, I'm not saying that,' I placated her, and she quickly mellowed.

When we landed, Dahlia took my hand and would not let go. She remained firmly attached all the way through customs and baggage reclaim. Since his daughter was fastened to me, her father and I, bewildered, had to strike up an awkward conversation. I hadn't noticed on the plane, with Dahlia all in my face, but he was strikingly handsome and very tall. His skin was a deep tan brown, and his eyes were grey-blue like an ocean the day after a hurricane. He was Cuban, from la Isla de la Juventud. I mentioned I'd been to Cuba. To Havana, Santiago, and a few places in between, but never to his comma-shaped, pine tree-covered homeland. 'You must visit one day,' he said. When it finally came time for us to part, Dahlia and her father to the taxis and me to my train, she kept turning around and waving until out of sight. 'I love you!' she hollered, from the other end of arrivals. 'I love you!'

THE HOPE, THE PRAYER, AND THE ANTHEM (OR, THE FALL SO FAR)
Rémy Ngamije

Okay. Listen. This is how it's going to go, kid: in a week's time you'll be thirty, and there's nothing you can do about it.

Thirty.

The age when, according to Franco, Rinzlo, Lindo, and Cicero—your homies—you'll be cast in your final form.

'No more evolutions,' Franco said gloomily.

'Pokémon to Pokéman and that's that.' Rinzlo, more certain than certain.

'Only sucks if you're spending your thirties alone,' Cicero said matter-of-factly.

Lindo saw you look away. 'Too soon, Cic,' he said.

Much too soon.

—An extract from your diary when reality hit: *30.* Jesus. Fucking. Christ!

At twenty, with life figured out in the special way literature undergrads have, you said at thirty you'd be headlining literary events around the world. There'd be rumours of an affair between you and Zadie Smith. The literary establishment would bay for her book, eager to see if she went full Alanis Morissette on you or partial

Adele. You'd never confirm or deny the tryst, smiling secretively at Hay Festival panels.

After your first pieces showed up in *Granta*, your debut novel—a contemporary street tale bristling with boyhood bravado—would pay the rent. The second book, some historically inspired story of a liberation struggle hero, would mark you as one of the continent's literati, well on your way to ticking your way down the shopping list of success compiled for you when you were born. This one, your parents decided as they held you, was touched by destiny.

That's why they named you The Way, The Goal, The Destination On The Horizon.

They dreamed of you when dreams were all they could afford, back when they lived in the Small Country. Your mother typed away at breakneck speed in an office somewhere; your father hustled over-the-counter medication. They met at the sweaty discotheque with the flickering blue fluorescent lighting, their eyes drawn to each other like opposing magnetic poles. From the first funky hip-shake to the Cornelius Brothers and Sister Rose's 'Too Late To Turn Back Now', they were promised to each other.

He said she danced like she was proposing to him. She said he danced like he accepted. He said, 'Yes.'

She said she didn't ask. She didn't have to: he was bought goods.

As he walked her home, the humidity gave them feverish sheens. His face glowed from the dancing; her cheekbones shone with delight at his presence. At her place, she kissed his cheek and watched him walk into the darkness, the equatorial night swallowing his ebony physique. She thought him a dream until he showed up at her work the next day. Everyone darted glances at him as he walked between the aisles to her desk. She drew him onto the balcony.

When would he see her again?

'Soon,' she said.

'Forever would be better.'

She laughed. 'Forever would be nice.'

They emerged from her village's church, married, showered with ululations. You hovered in their hearts when they bought their first house, when they buried her mother, and his father. Your mother wanted a baby. He said, 'Me too.'

'A boy,' she said. 'With your smile.'

'Or a girl,' he said. 'With your eyes.'

They'd be happy with the womb's lottery: a healthy baby made from the best parts of them.

They prayed for you after her first miscarriage. They weren't believers, but they prayed every day for nine months when she fell pregnant again. Their enemies were banned from the house lest any bad energy seeped into her womb and turned you against life. Your father rushed home from work to press his head against her stomach. Your mother shooed him away. He joked that his job was a ploy to keep you to herself. 'It's only fair,' she said. 'If it's a boy, it will be a matter of time before he outgrows me and I become an embarrassing nuisance. I might have more time with a girl before a boy takes her away too.' Your familiar weight and how it made people treat her differently, your father's reverential protection and provision—she didn't want to relinquish the status you brought her.

You wanted out.

Out you came—the First Sundering—painfully, bloody.

Finally.

They prepared a room and a home: for your first day of school and your achievements, for your freedom and the Second Sundering—a wife and grandchildren. They readied themselves for these things from the moment you breathed and screamed.

When they could prepare no more they simply hoped in the way only people who know what it is to lose can hope. All you know is the one hope they ever voiced, to be what they yearned to be most when they were in search of refuge: safe and landed, the owner of things.

The owner of permanent and inheritable things.

Not to worry, you told them: title deeds would follow your great deeds.

First: a modern house in a manicured suburb fond of recycling. Second: a wife (quarter Venezuelan, two-thirds Eritrean, three-sixteenths Themysciran Amazon). Third: twin daughters with curls casting agents killed for (Harvard on the horizon for the eldest, a future human rights lawyer; Cambridge for the younger progeny, another writer in the family).

Then the third acclaimed novel: something about complicated parenthood and the gear changes of interracial marriages.

Praise for the Third Novel:

'A magisterial, perspicacious, and layered story which self-assuredly explores the pitfalls of modern marriage while affirming the enduring promise of love.' —Publishers Weekly

'The voice of a continent.' —Some Important Literary Figure

Ah. Look at you.

I SAY I SAID *LOOKATEW!*

A residency in New York (the epicentre of the Zadie Smith affair) would yield the fourth multiple award-winning Afro-American tale: slaves and gold from Ghana; colonialism in the Congo; diaspora, drugs, and detention in the US, all topped with an earth-shattering romance between Some Black Guy and Some White Woman. It would astound audiences everywhere, lay siege to *The New York Times* bestseller list like a Mongol army come to reshape the geopolitics of the world—the book quoted for intellectual points.

Who could've known a boy from the Small Country, raised in the wide and dry New Country, could climb so high? Your neighbourhood was known for its dedication to beer, biltong, battery, teenage pregnancies, and souped-up STI Golfs revving from gonorrhoea to HIV in sex seconds flat. Readers like you were treated like lepers, shunned from the dust-patch soccer games with biblical fastidiousness.

You always knew.

For *kontrol* you'd purchase a farm in the New Country, some unimaginably large landmass stolen from a long-ago massacred indigenous tribe. Your old man would retire there to feign feudal interest in farming. His grief would finally unwind itself from his neck, fall to the ground, slither away into the undergrowth, sprouting feet and arms as it went along, a beautiful black face with close-cropped hair, and a radiant gap-toothed smile. It would hold you in its patient gaze.

'*Komeza,*' it would say before fading away.

Carry on.

You'd say, 'Yes, Mamma. I will.'

Your father would breathe deeply, from the wrinkled skin on his forehead down to his toes, and let out the throaty laugh he stowed away as he crushed your hand in his at the funeral, leaning on you for support. Your younger brother was nearby, but it was upon you his full weight rested. The first thump of soil on the coffin nearly made you faint. The grave felt like a Charybdis capable of devouring the universe, flushing creation from this life into the next—a Final Sundering. But on the farm which stretched from East to West a sun would rise without its mourning glory. Your father would find peace. In the autumnal sunset on this farm of farms you'd whittle away at a possible memoir. There'd be tours to plan, lectures to prepare, awards to adjudicate, grants to graciously accept.

—Your cursive vow before The Fall: *9 years and 358 days to greatness.*

At twenty-seven you were still plugged into the club scene. The fatigue showed. One time, at this moist joint, a light-skinned item with eyebrows from YouTube and hair from Peru chatted you up. You stepped outside so she could smoke. She said she liked the song thumping through the walls. You said music was eating itself: everything was a cover of a remix—you used the word *pastiche*.

'You sound like an old ass nigga.' Her weave Nike-swished away.

You knew Pink when she had pink hair and made R&B jams. You and Enrique Iglesias threw back to 'Bailamos' before he ditched the mole.

You were a yoof no longer.

You started evening art classes to pass the time and left them because some artsy fool you hated from the first brushstroke called one of your pieces pastiche. Everyone agreed. Even the Coloured girl whose work would be at home in Oscar The Grouch's dustbin on Sesame Street. (She's exhibiting at MoMA soon.) The two of you might have had something before she agreed with Dude Who Actually Paints Well And Kind Of Has A Point But Fuck Him And His Family Back To Adam And Eve.

—Your observation when you forfeited a future in the Louvre: *Art is the bread of life, artists are the gluten—that shit isn't for everyone.*

Next distraction: dancing at the salsa club at the end of the world, a lonely outpost of rhythm. Your boys laughed at you. You didn't care. You had to try new things before this snow globe city drove you mad. You were going to *cumbia* the shit out of that dance floor. The Buena Vista Social Club's 'Chan Chan' became your ringtone. You practised *ochos* while you seasoned your two-minute noodles and scrambled eggs, dreaming about slo-mo walking into a San Juan club with Hector Lavoe's 'La Murga' as your soundtrack, announcing the arrival of *El Salsero Del Desierto*, the high noon cowboy and melody mercenary come to clear out the riff-raff and guns in the valley.

The salsa bug lasted until the Spanish girl in your classes swatted your balls away from her wickets for a soft six instead of hard sex. She was in the country doing volunteer work in the *lokasie* and didn't know anything or anyone in the Oh-Six-One. Sparked, you took her to *braais*, hikes, and Spoken Word performances.

She said she'd never seen *The Godfather* trilogy.

'GERRARRAHEEYA!'

You had the trilogy at home. Her suggestion: meet up, practise salsa, cook, and watch the films, alternate between your places.

Three nights with the dark-eyed *mariposa* who struggled with timing and—*Dios mio*—couldn't execute an outside turn without taking out half the dance floor? 'Si,' you said.

Si! Si! Si!

The first night you made a stir-fry with meats unknown, an offer you said she couldn't refuse. (Earlier, when she'd texted she was en route, you busted out Celia Cruz—'*O! Yeah, come over!*'—but she didn't get it.) The second night, for *Part II*, she made pasta *Alfredo*. (You wisely decided not to use the quip.) On the third, your last home game, you teamed up for a joint hurrah and made gnocchi. After the end credits, you sat and decided to run DMC game on her by having a deep meaningful conversation. The expanding universe with its Neil DeGrasse Tyson film spoiler-physics told you to kiss the girl but *sha-la-la-la-la-la my oh my* she put a gentle hand on your chest and said no. *Muchos apologiendos* later—you insisted on making up Spanish around her—she hoped you'd remain friends.

You skipped classes, avoiding her. Then, one day, she showed up with a dreadlocked, earthy-smelling, tour guide boyfriend. You were on Duolingo for this Catalonian *blanquita*, and she went full native on your ass.

Mierda!

The salsa studio saved you the embarrassment of quitting by finishing its last dance with rent rates higher than a Californian rapper: it closed and didn't reopen. Franco and the guys said *cero y nada* about you being king of the Oh-Sex-None for gassing the Spanish girl's pursuit.

This wasn't the end for you, kid.

Couldn't be. Wouldn't be. *No fucking way.*

Twenty-eight would be the *año* of writing. All you needed was some cultured inspiration.

Cue birding. For a month you enthused about crimson-breasted shrikes and martial eagles. But bird-watching was a bar of boredom so high you couldn't Fosbury flop over it. Instead, you hit the gym like draft day was approaching. Twice a day, six days of the week, waking up at fuck-me five o'clock for cardio and then hitting the weights in the evening until the cleaning staff came to wipe your sweat off the benches before taking their midnight taxis back to the hood. Gym was a different kind of church: form was faith, reps were religion, sets were sacraments. The ensuing female attention was crazy. You chewed through them like Pac-Man with three bonus lives. Given the country's VIP status on the WHO's HIV/AIDS indices, it's a miracle you didn't eat a ghost and die. Some women hoped they'd hit the jackpot with you, pulling on your lever. I—*yank*—Love—*yank*—Y—*your hands and what they do to me!* You swallowed their emotional pennies and told them to have another go.

Playing the game put the worst parts of you on blast and repeat.

—Your retirement speech when you hung up your player jersey: *Pussy is a destabilising force, like oil in a West African country.*

Franco said you were making a mistake: 'Trust me, if life's willing to hold the head steady, you gotta milk the cow.'

Nah. You gave it all up. The only things you'd sleep with, you said, were books, working through the literary canon. But, fuck,

James Joyce was a trial, and Tolstoy was a chore. (You finished *War and Peace*, though, and enjoyed letting people know you did.) You gave the classics a skip. You'd try them later when you were famous, when you had time to make time.

The writing?

Ha! There was always a distraction. Like the needlessly competitive pickup basketball games. Once, you drove for the hoop, hit Lindo with the wettest Shammgod, finger-rolled for a stylish two points, and landed funny. You were in pain for days. The doctor's diagnosis prescribed a road trip to Cape Town for special surgery. You knew it wasn't happening—you didn't have medical aid. You were no Ray Allen, and with your layup game shot to shit, you could keep the failing construction industry supplied with cheap bricks. Windhoek, you decided, was a city of old men with diseases and young men with injuries. You sighed your way to the bench, playing every other weekend to save your bad knee.

Soon you'll be too old for any under-thirty list. The student newspaper you started at your high school profiled cool, young teachers and you didn't make the cut. You failed a couple of senior essays out of spite.

You have no girl. The One departed a year ago. Because she was lovely, and because you anointed her as The One, you ache for her on cold days when there's a spiteful breeze in the air.

She was something too, something real: stretch marks on a booty which registered the tiniest hiccup of the Eurasian Plate, a Care Bear hug that warmed from the inside out, and toes so cute they reconciled arguments (you could never apologize to people with ugly toes). She chose a restaurant meal quicker than a Jamaican sprinter broke a world record and improved your knowledge of obscure herbs and spices. Your attempts at replicating her tarragon fish long after she'd pulled herself ashore from the maelstrom of your breakup reminded you what a catch she was. You whimpered for her, a fiend fighting withdrawal.

Unlike the other *cherries* van die Laeveld, Kloppersdal, or Donkerhoek—who said Jesus, Chuck Taylor, and Jack Purcell were the only men who'd never let them down—your girl wasn't impressed by Imprezzas. Girls from those blurry margins between hoods graduated into women in the back of boys' cars when puberty peaked through their blouses. When she let you take her out on a date ('It must be public—I don't want to be in a place where only you can hear me say no.') she didn't negotiate with her dignity. 'The price of all of this,' she said, 'is all of you. All of the time.'

When you curled up behind her in bed, all you smelled was shea butter and coconut oil. You squirmed from that thing she did with her finger. Her pussy was hotter than a pan of oil and had possum power—you played dead for an hour after hitting it, leaving your sheets looking like Jackson Pollocks. Get this: you let her handle your *Yu-Gi-Oh* cards. In your shady womb raider past, you'd dive into vulvas in the back of Volvos *inyama kwa nyama*, but you *never* let anyone touch your cards. She asked if it was a sign you were ready to talk about more than surface things. You said you were, sneak-peeking her trailers of the life to come. She said you were motivated by faith, even if you'd never admit to it—that if you believed in something you didn't shift from the goal. Your conviction, she said, would make you a good father. You couldn't get it up for two weeks after that. You, the man with a dick harder than an end-level boss. (Her words, not yours.)

Why?

You were scared you'd make her a mother and didn't want to get into the habit of losing them. You saw what it did to your father. He shuffled from home to work and work to home, husked out, thinned, colder than zero, lonelier than the loneliest hero.

Fourteen days of your girlfriend asking if everything was okay. Fourteen nights of you telling her everything was fine, afraid if you took her to bed you'd go from Smash Bro to Splash Brother, shooting fatherhood and till death do us part into her ovaries with Curry-esque abandon. On the fifteenth day you managed to squeeze a semi into her.

She thought it was something she did, or something she wasn't doing.

You wondered how to tell her about the hollowness which silenced you in her comforting company; about your belly button, throbbing, aching for that distant First Sundering; or the alien sadness inside you which ripped through your chest and preyed on your world. You remained silent and kept your shields at sixty-five percent—strong enough to keep her questions at bay, weak enough to make her feel like she'd wear them down to zero and receive an answer that wasn't the press release you gave everyone else: okay, cool, no worries, all good, aight. You, my friend, were a slow puncture of love. Even when the ride stopped, she got out and pushed a little longer. Then, finally, your mother's absence showed up with the pull of a collapsed star. No light or hope could escape its event horizon.

You sat her down, looking at the start in her; she saw the end in you.

You did that thing where you said you didn't deserve her. She did that Destiny's Child thing where she realized you didn't. She went Sub-Zero cold, fatality-kicked your ass out of her Earth Realm, an exile so catatonic you lost five kilograms. Her next man would listen to her talking about you, wondering how you managed to lose her. You knew all of this because you were *that guy* who sat down with her on Day One Of Forever listening to her talk about her fumbling exes. A month ago you saw her at the mall and ducked into a plus-size shop, watching her walk by the store's window while you pretended to peruse the skirts.

She's in Costa Rica now. Her Instagram is full of curved beaches and green trees. She's drenched in sunlight you said you'd see together. You can't see it in her pictures but you have this intestine-twisting feeling the person holding her camera phone is some Alejandro who protects her heart and puts such a furious dicking on her she forgets you ever existed.

That was a year ago.

You're 29, fam. You have *fokol* paperback to your name.

So, what do you do?

You flick through your diary for the wisdom you'd share with the *The Paris Review: Writing is confession.*

You add another: *Reading is some kind of forgiveness.*

That is your hope, prayer, and anthem.

You summon the courage to record the fall so far:

Okay. Listen. This is how it's going to go, kid: in a week's time you'll be thirty and there's nothing you can do about it.

GRACIOUS
Faraaz Mahomed

We buried my mother in a quiet corner of the Klip Road Cemetery, near a sneezewood tree that cast a crooked shadow in the middle of the day. If she was standing upright, she'd have been able to gaze in on her flat in Grassy Park.

My brother Moegsien still lives there, in the bedroom we shared when we were children. Anyone looking at the walls closely enough would see the outlines of old Sellotape stains where our posters of BMW M1s and N.W.A. used to be. He sleeps in the same bed that he used to before he went to Pollsmoor Prison, like someone who's stopped attempting any other life.

As the cancer ate into my mother's colon, and her body weakened and bent like a sapling in a storm, she would clutch onto her tasbih, mouthing words to herself between thin and wrinkled lips that each day seemed to become more purple, until one day they were the colour of the grapes in the Constantia vineyards.

'Inna lillahi wa'inna ilayhi raji'oon.'

We are from Allah, and we will return to Allah. When my mother did die, Moegsien, our sister Sawligha, and I grimaced through the *gadats* for a few weeks, greeting old uncles, collecting condolences like they were *eid* money, remembering, between the three of us, her guttural laugh and the silly jitterbug dances she did to cheer us up when we were sick.

I first met Bertha about a month after my mother died. She was waiting outside the lecture hall, golden blond hair atop a head that tilted upward as she read a poster on the notice board. I didn't pay much attention to her because I was talking to one of my students about his paper, pointing out how he'd misunderstood some aspects of the burden of proof in the Employment Equity Act.

I only vaguely recognized her as the woman in the corridor when she came to my office. She had a timid knock like she was pre-apologizing for what she was about to do next. I didn't invite her in immediately, instead sticking my head out in the aperture between the open door and the frame.

'Hi, Professor Badat?'

'Yes, that's me.'

'My name is Bertha Steyn. I was wondering if we could talk about something?'

Her words felt hesitant, like they were peeping out from behind a shield.

'Can you tell me what this is about? I'm in the middle of marking papers.'

When she mentioned my mother, I felt a sudden piercing that travelled through my body. I let her in, hoping she was just there to settle something about my mother's retirement money, accumulated from years of cleaning the halls of Parliament. When I was really young, I would go with her sometimes, on a Sunday or a holiday, and I'd look up at waxy pictures of old men or pass the time by counting the earth-coloured tiles on the floor.

Bertha sat uncomfortably, her ankles together and the grey-blue centres of her eyes trained on me. She was a tallish woman, but she was stooped low in the seat, curving like a two-day-old moon. She told me in short and nervous sentences that she was the daughter of Carl Lamprecht, one of the MPs for the Nats when we were growing up. He'd been a stoic supporter of Group Areas, a keen proponent of 'separate but equal'.

When she started to unclench, Bertha said that she used to be a teacher too. She taught music at Wynberg Boys but retired early to try her hand at painting. And then she told me, with a pregnant pause, that she was my sister.

Our house in Pinelands is on a quiet street not far from the town hall. We found it when my daughter, Asma, was six because we thought we might want to have another child. The white wall needs repainting often because it gets beaten with sunshine, and sometimes, we find pieces of the thatch from the roof in the driveway.

My wife, Aisha, and I were sitting in the dining room, with steam rising from a pot of soup, when I told her about Bertha. She was appalled. She didn't know who she was angry at, so it was really just a patchwork of words that sprayed like a leaking hose. I was angry too.

'What does this woman want?'

'I really don't know.'

'But she wants something right?'

'I hope not. I'm not really inclined to give her anything, especially considering who she is.'

'*Genade!* Gracious!'

Aisha came with me when we went to have our blood tested. She looked Bertha up and down like an X-ray, searching for signs that we were related. Bertha showed us the letter from Carl. It was worn and frayed, with handwriting so slanted that it looked like it was being shoved by a gale. The paper was a faded yellow, and the words were a sallow blue.

She told us it was given to her by her aunt, Carl's sister, who died, just a week before my mother did, from cancer of the throat, maybe from all the unspoken secrets that were cratered inside. The letter didn't say much about what happened. It was just a recounting, a stony collection of facts about my parentage.

Aisha and I read it three times over, looking for an indication of their relationship, for some sign of shame or guilt or affection. There was none. There was only a residue of something that was and then wasn't.

My siblings used to call me *Witbooi* sometimes. They laughed at the fact that I used to read Faulkner and liked to play cricket. Moegsien liked to say that my nose was too long, that my skin was too pale, or that the way I walked reminded him of someone from Rondebosch. He would mock me, imitating my steps with an exaggerated bob, tip-tap, laughing as he told me that I was someone else's brother.

Our father, Shuaib, was a short man with a soft voice and a pained expression. He worked long hours as a security guard at the day hospital, saving up for me to go to university.

'I want to become a doctor, a surgeon.'

'You should become a lawyer, maybe an advocate—'

'Why?'

'Our people need more lawyers. *Hulle sal altyd vir ons kom.*'

They'll always be coming for us, he said, with an ember of struggle in his words. He talked about the day in 1976 when they made them move to Grassy Park, suitcases in hand while the beady-eyed policemen stood watching with their hands on their holsters. Sometimes he would say that he wanted us to move back to District Six. Then maybe, he thought, Moegsien would be fine, not a lazy and unhappy person pretending to be a hardened gangster.

'*Inshallah.*'

He liked to say Inshallah, if God wills, and he liked to say

Alhamdulillah, all praise is due to God alone. In fact, I think that was the last word I heard him say. He died when I was thirty, keeled over from a massive heart attack one morning at the kitchen table. His face landed in a half-eaten bowl of cornflakes. We tried to call an ambulance, but it never came.

When I was certain that Carl was my biological father, I went to see Moegsien and asked Sawligha to come from Muizenberg. It was a Sunday afternoon; Sawligha was tired and short. Moegsien's face was ghostly. He twitched intermittently and spoke in brief remarks peppered with shivers and tics.

'*Ek wil jou iets vertel.*'

'*Ja,* so tell us,' she said.

'There's a woman, Bertha Steyn, that came to see me a few weeks ago.'

I told them about the blood test and the letter. It led to a series of anxious questions that I didn't know the answers to. I wasn't sure if they'd had a prolonged affair or a quick encounter. I wasn't sure how our mother felt, if she was scared or pressured or intoxicated by Carl. I didn't know if my father, Shuaib that is, knew.

I was hoping that we would process the information together, sharing a mind as we worked out what it all meant. They didn't say anything about being upset or even suggest to me that things were different. But their silence was suggestion enough. The news hadn't landed in front of us; it had landed between us.

My mother's tasbih was hung precariously by the corner of an ornamental frame with the name of Allah at the entrance. It rattled whenever there were footsteps. As I left that day, it splayed to the floor like a heavy raindrop.

I drove past the cemetery to go home. I didn't stop; I just said a quick hello. Moegsien was at the window as I drove off, his drug-addled face mouthing nothings to himself.

* * *

I went to Bertha's house for the first time on a Saturday morning in May. The wind kept trying to shove my car sidewards on the M5. She lived at the top of a small hill in Hout Bay. The house looked like it was on a cliff edge.

When I got there, she seemed very different to the person I'd met before, less reticent, more alive. Her blonde hair was swept back but flecks of it kept rushing across her face because their house was unprotected from the force of the late southeaster.

There was a faint, shallow sound of water crashing into itself outside as we sat in her kitchen and sipped on tea. I was starting to see little traces of myself in her, in the way her lips curled into a jagged smile and the way her forehead creased like mushy clay.

Her family was lovely and welcoming. She had three daughters, two of whom were still living at home. The eldest was becoming a pastry chef in Paris. Her husband, Paul, was blond too, with an inkling of an Afrikaans accent underneath his boardroom voice. He was an engineer at the docks and a rugby player.

We made tentative plans for Aisha and Asma to come over and meet the cousins, and we watched their *boerboel* chase after butterflies in their garden. He would've fallen over the hill had there not been a fence.

She showed me her paintings, mostly of faces close up, in bright colours that clashed against each other. One was a self-portrait rendered in glowing reds and yellows. Her skin was bronze, and her hair looked like a restless flame.

'You have a real talent.'

'I'm not sure. I think there's something missing from them.'

She was right. They felt lifeless, but I didn't want to say that. Afterwards, we sat in her living room and shared stories about our families. I asked Bertha about our father.

'He was a stern man. He loved God.'

'Ah,' I said, 'that's ironic.'

Her body shifted like it was being uprooted from the ground. To change the subject, she talked about growing up in Newlands, with a wispy fondness that didn't match how I felt about Grassy Park, and about her brothers. There were two, Jacques, who lived in Woodstock, and Peter, who lived in Walvis Bay. It was in the late afternoon, when the day was fallow and darkening, that she told me about Jacques's acute lymphoblastic leukaemia.

A thin coating formed on her cheeks from a handful of tears. She told me that neither she nor Peter was a tissue match.

Aisha, Bertha, and I went to see Jacques and his partner André in Woodstock the following weekend. He had the same pearly eyes and lilting voice as Bertha, but I couldn't really see myself in him. He was friendly, in a distant and hesitant way. Aisha was cordial even though she'd questioned my decision to meet Jacques and was discouraging of any consideration of surgery. She complimented the mural of Table Mountain in the clouds that Andre had painted.

'You're a family of painters!' Even I didn't know if she was being caustic.

I was unaware, but Jacques taught English Literature at the university, three buildings away from my office. In fact, he was in the middle of a tutorial on Tayari Jones when the voicemail from his doctors came in. He said he sat in his office for two hours after he played the message that day. His frailty felt like more than a product of cancer. He felt like a delicate person, like porcelain.

There was an old picture of Carl sitting on the windowsill, housed in a faded brass frame. He was speaking in Parliament, pressing the fingers of his two hands against each other like I sometimes do when I'm lecturing. His face was bullish, confident. As I glanced at it, I thought to myself that I had the same rough edges, like a piece of carelessly torn paper.

André was slick and handsome. He spoke quickly, and he fidgeted a lot. While we sat with Jacques, he went into the kitchen and, a few minutes later, brought out a curry made with snoek. He lifted his eyebrows at us as if to say that he'd made it specially for us.

It tasted bland, like white people's curry, but we praised it anyway as the four of us ate while Jacques stared at his reflection in the broth in his bowl.

'I really appreciate you doing this,' Jacques said to me.

I wasn't sure how to respond. I hadn't agreed to do anything.

'The test I mean . . . Bertha said that—'

Aisha shot Bertha a glare.

'He hasn't decided.'

Bertha looked at me with pleading eyes.

'Oh . . . we were . . . we thought that . . . we just thought that you were going to do it.'

Before we came, I thought I would do it too. It felt like it was the generous thing to do. But their assumption made me feel conflicted.

'I think we can talk about that after lunch.'

André became agitated and readied to say something. Jacques put his hand on Andre's arm to calm him down. Aisha was roiled.

'You can't possibly expect that he would have surgery for somebody he's just met, for a Nat *nogal. Die mense,*' she said to me, pointing a finger at Jacques. She didn't finish what she was about to say.

There was a vacant silence after that, punctuated by the sound of our chewing and by Bertha's unsuccessful attempt at holding back tears.

As André collected our plates, Bertha looked at me.

'I wish I could undo the things my father did. But Jacques is not my father.'

My body turned to her, tight like a fist.

'Don't you mean our father?'

The hospital had whitewashed walls, and the corridors surrounded a rectangular courtyard behind shuttered doors and windows. Asma was scared even though we'd explained to her that the procedure had a minuscule chance of complications. Her hand cupped into Aisha's like halves of a mussel shell, and they stood in the waiting room as Jacques and I were wheeled away. His eyes caught mine while we waited for the lift. I still couldn't see myself in him.

A giant needle bored into the back of my pelvis, and I felt it burrow into me. It felt like I was being invaded, but I was so knocked up that I could only sense the strangeness of it and not the pain. They incised the bone while I was half-conscious, while I watched shoes covered with shower caps dance around me.

My mother's face appeared, young and comely, proud. She was holding her tasbih, muttering prayers to herself. There was a haze, and it kept her from seeing me. I looked around for my father, Shuaib that is. I could see a pair of feet underneath a cloud, clad in brown leather lace-ups, standing firmly on rubbly gravel like they were at attention. I wasn't sure whose feet they were.

I thought they were in Grassy Park, but then I heard a few whistles, like sirens, blaring from nowhere. It wasn't Grassy Park. A suitcase appeared, and there was mad shouting in a language I couldn't understand. I didn't need the language to understand the meaning.

I heard a loud bleep, and I felt my eyes flutter.

My back, butt, and legs were sore when I awoke, and my mouth tasted like there'd been a blanket shoved inside it. Without reason, the first thought that came to my mind was the Employment Equity Act and the burden of proof for unfair discrimination.

Light was encasing Sawligha's face as she stood over me, and Aisha's hand clutched onto mine tightly. The anaesthetic was clouding everything, making my body not feel like my body. Bertha smiled at me from the doorway, a fulsome smile like one of her paintings. Moegsien didn't come. I texted him to say I was okay, and he replied a few days later.

'Alhamdulillah.'

For a while after the surgery, Bertha would call to invite us over, saying that she wanted her girls to meet Asma. Aisha was wholly against it. Sometimes there was a feral glow in her eyes when the subject of my 'other family' came up.

I received a couple of messages about Jacques's health. He was recovering, but slowly and with a lot of pain and weakness. Once, Bertha sent a picture of the two of them. The hollow ridges in Jacques's face and the exhausted fear in his eyes reminded me of the last few times I saw my mother.

I hadn't spoken to Moegsien for a while, so I drove to Grassy Park to see him one day. It was getting to Spring, so the windows of the flats were all open and the curtains all blew outward like they wanted to escape but were being held back by the burglar bars.

He was always thin, but his body looked like a sausage casing that had shed its meat. He seemed dazed and irritable, and a yellow film covered his eyes.

'How are you?'

He still had a slight limp in his gait from the gunshot wound in his leg. Along with his missing teeth, they were like beacons from the past, from the day he tried to rob the liquor store in Capricorn, from his life in prison.

With a huff in his voice, he told me that he wasn't working at the petrol station anymore, that he'd lost his job. He was quiet for a while and then he said he could get another job through his friend Baboo.

'What kind of job?'

He didn't like the questions. I could see from the kink in his brow that he felt like he was being scolded.

'Jy's nie my pa nie.'

I wasn't his father, he said. I didn't have any right to ask him these questions. He was jittery, like an anxious puppy running on the flats, trying to get away from its angry owner, trying to not be the dog in 'kick the dog'.

'Ek will net hoor dat . . . I just want to hear that you're okay.'

He stood up and went to look out the window. We could both see the shaking branches of the sneezewood tree, but only Moegsien could see our mother's grave.

I heard a brief whimper, just a momentary spurt of mournful sound that seemed to ask my mother an unanswerable question.

'Ek is fine.'

We took Asma to the Ferris Wheel at the Waterfront during the school holidays. It was loud and there was a crush of energetic children all waiting to have a go. Aisha had bought us all ice cream, so we stood in the line and lapped at our cones. With the heat of the sun, it started to dribble down our hands and towards our elbows. A few drops of cocoa coloured liquid landed in between the pink and blue flowers on Asma's otherwise white dress.

'Genade!'

Asma licked her own bare arms while Aisha searched inside her handbag for tissues. When she didn't find any, I went to the toilets to get some.

It was a longish walk, past the throng at the food court. I had to weave through a few bodies and my shoulders bumped into people. The door of the men's room swung wildly and almost knocked into me. I took a step back, and when the door opened, I saw Jacques's anaemic face.

We exchanged greetings and pleasantries and then I asked him how he was feeling.

'I'm definitely . . . I can't thank you enough.'

His voice cracked, and he leaned towards me to give me a hug. It caught me by surprise, but I didn't resist.

'I know it's a bit complicated, but I want you to come over again.'

He seemed sincere, sweet even, so I told him I would. I think I even wanted to.

When I got back to the wheel, they'd gone up already. I could see Asma's face and her hands pressed against the plastic of the pod. She was watching the crowd below, scanning through it. She jumped a little when she saw me and waved her hands eagerly like there was smoke in front of her face.

Later, we drove down the N2 to go home. It had just gone past five o'clock when we were passing District Six, and so the *athaan* was blaring for the *Asr salaah* from the minaret of the Zonnebloem mosque. Its cadence was steep like the cliffside of the mountain. The first *'Allahu-akbar'* called out bashfully, and then, a moment later, the second exploded violently into the sky, with the clamour of ten thousand police whistles.

BLACKIE
Yop Dalyop

Mama's thighs squished my head. I could feel her protruding tummy if I leaned too far back. My buttocks felt numb on the cool tiles from hours of sitting, and her knees kept my head in place as she braided my hair. I shrieked whenever she tugged hard at my hair, and the cracking of my dry scalp made my headache worse. She used *mayang* oil to soothe the pain, but the rich, nutty, and smoky smell of the palm kernel oil made me gag.

Three weeks ago, she left the hair relaxer in too long.

As she conversed with one of her clients about the foods her catering company could offer, Mama would look at me every ten minutes then ask, 'Is it burning you yet?' I shook my head from side to side and continued my writing even though it felt like little needles were dancing on my scalp, from the back of my head to the front. I was already done with the essay Miss Martha gave as holiday homework when my older sister, Aniebie, screamed for Mama's attention. I knew it was serious because Mama dragged me to her bathroom. We never used Mama's bathroom. It was always sparkling clean and smelled of Dettol antiseptic. But my head hung in the bathtub she washed every day, and as her fingers worked through my once thick and full hair, limp straight moulds of hair went down the drain. I didn't cry when I saw patches that once had thick coils. I didn't cry when Aniebie's dread-filled face tried to stay straight. But I couldn't hold back the tears when Mama asked: 'Why didn't you tell me it was burning you?'

I was wrapped in a towel while Aniebie kept her arms around me in an attempt to provide comfort. I shouldn't have struggled as she held me, but I couldn't help the anger that made my insides feel like I'd just eaten a peppery meal. To me, it was Aniebie's fault Mama decided to relax my hair. Why did she have to have the kind of hair that didn't shrink in fear? Why did her hair always appear so long?

Mama made my hair in my room instead of the kitchen to make sure hair didn't 'fly' into pots of food. We were expecting Grandma, and it would be bad if she were to see hair on the floor or in her food. I didn't have the time to worry about my hair because the neatly ironed pinafore and shirt hung on the handle of my dresser reminded me that the holidays had come to an end. Unlike Aniebie, I didn't spend time twirling around in front of the mirror in my new uniform and shoes. When I tried on my uniform, I pulled at the shirt to make sure the chest area didn't appear too tight. But it felt smaller each month, and my growing chest became more apparent. This year wasn't like any other. My classroom wouldn't have Miss Martha in it all the time. I was finally going to use ink pens in class rather than pencils, and the stripes on the uniform, which resembled Aniebie's, distinguished from the primary school pupils.

When Mama finished braiding my hair, I could see dried flakes from my scalp, but my hair was bone straight when I looked in the mirror. It didn't stand up or puff in every direction. It wasn't as voluminous as before, but it fell past my shoulders in neat braids just like Aniebie's. It was now straight, and I knew that once Grandma arrived, she would say my hair was good.

The dark green car Grandma came in almost touched the ground because of the weight of all the goods in it. The trunk had yams poking out from it, with a long green rope tied across the tubers to stop them from falling. The front seat had fresh palm kernels and bunches of *afang* and *ugu* leaves that I imagined would've obstructed the driver's view of the side mirror. The back seat had mangoes, peppers, and tomatoes on the floor and a bag of dried shrimps with dried fish that added flavour to soups.

The woody, sweet smell of the village engulfed me when Grandma hugged me tightly. My cheek was against the itchy lace material she wore, but I took every second to breathe in the scent of the village I missed. Within Grandma's embrace, I remembered our car being chased by happy children the first time we visited the village. I remembered watching older women extract mayang oil from the hard palm kernel nuts with clay pots heated by dried palm leaves and firewood.

We didn't go to the village much after Ete Ima's mysterious death. Although it was six years ago, Grandma still believed ninety-two-year-old Grandpa would have lived longer if he hadn't shared a meal with his troublesome brother after a squabble over land. Grandma pulled back to examine my face. She placed her warm unwashed wet hands around my beaming face as she was accustomed to, then spoke. 'My love, you've grown so much, but so dark now.'

Grandma spun me around with her hands to examine my body carefully before speaking to Mama. 'Ini, she needs a bra.'

I was Grandma's love who had grown so much. I heard this at least once a month now. On hot afternoons when we lay on the living room floor sipping chilled, sweet hibiscus juice, Mama would say something out of the blue like, 'You grow tall overnight.' And if I wasn't seen reading at least once a day, Mama would say, 'Aniema, you aren't a small girl anymore. You're starting the seventh grade.'

Aniebie was Grandma's beauty, and Mama was her pride. None of those had changed since the last time Grandma saw us. Since

Papa's visit from the United States five months ago, Mama spent more time at home with her feet placed on the mahogany coffee table. We've had to get used to talking to Papa over the phone. He left for the United States after finding an even better job than the one he had at a popular oil company in our hometown of Uyo. We went to one of the best schools. We had a driver, three cars, a maid, and a four-bedroom house located in the island part of Lagos. But Papa told us our future would be more secure abroad than in Nigeria. In his words, 'It doesn't take inflated contracts to build a pot-holed road abroad.'

At first, it wasn't hard to cope with Papa's absence. He used to spend months away then come home to spend the holidays, but it became harder when church members asked about his absence and my classmates joked about my missing father. Papa filled up his absence with parcels containing new clothes, gifts, and handwritten letters for each of us. The most recent package contained vitamins for Mama, and Aniebie and I exchanged knowing looks when she hid it in her room. We did the same every evening at the dinner table when she would ask Uduak, our house help, to add more food to her plate, but we never dared say a thing about a baby. Talking about it brought bad luck. Two years ago, Mama bought a crib and would pick a pack of diapers every time we went to the supermarket. At night when I said my prayers to God, I would beg him to make the baby come faster so I could brush his hair and run baths. We had a large party for the baby and picked out a name for a boy. It had to be a boy. Mama already had two girls, and a boy would fit into our family perfectly.

But Mama got malaria and spent a week at the hospital. Papa didn't let us go to the hospital, relaying Mama's messages about being good to Aniebie and me. The night Mama returned from the hospital, her stomach drooped past her waist. Mama whose heels bounced while she walked, traipsed up the stairs. I stared at the dark sky with messy grey clouds thrown all over it and wondered if my prayers to God made him work too fast.

For weeks, Mama's once vibrant light skin looked pale, and she walked around the house like a lost visitor. But when Grandma came, she got better. Grandma forced Mama to eat like she did to us and massaged her with wet slabs of bentonite clay she brought from the village. Grandma was sure the baby died because of her enemies. I overheard her scolding Mama in the study about maternity pictures, baby showers, and ridiculous trends that disregarded culture. There was a reason our culture didn't broadcast a pregnancy. If our enemies came to know Mama was expecting, they would take away our joy. Uduak, who was well-versed in tradition, said it was true. She had an aunt who lost a child in the same manner.

But this time around, Grandma's visit wasn't to relay a sad message or to comfort Mama. She was here to take care of Mama until she gave birth. Uduak lowered her voice when she told Aniebie and me it was the custom for a mother to take care of her daughter until she gave birth. Uduak didn't try to hint at anything as she scraped the bottom of the pot with a spoon. It was just a fact she reminded us of. As I washed red soil from the yams off my palms in the kitchen, Uduak said it was also the custom to feed a pregnant woman with plenty food.

That night, the joy that bubbled from the bottom of my stomach was hard to keep bottled under my warm blanket. Aniebie lay under me on the bottom bunk, and I could hear her say her prayers through the silent hum of the air conditioner. Ever since we lost the baby, I couldn't bring myself to pray. Each night, I waited for Aniebie to pray, then I whispered an amen loud enough for just me to hear. After my silent amen I said, 'Mama is pregnant.' The words were awfully familiar, and I bit on my bottom lip as if to caution it until Aniebie said something. All she did was sigh.

* * *

The thin metal dug into my shoulders, and I used my hands to shield the prying eyes of Grandma, Mama, Uduak, and Aniebie as I put on the new bra Grandma bought for me. The red living room curtains were my makeshift fitting room. I looked at my vague reflection in the glass window; my chest wasn't pointy with the well-rounded bra on, but my shoulders ached from the tension.

'What are you hiding? I'm your grandma.'

Grandma fiddled with both straps, and from time to time, to know if the tension was right, she would let go of one of the straps causing it to slap my shoulder. I stared at the fluffy milk-coloured carpet I often lay on to do my homework, but its threads now felt like grease between my toes. It was just two years ago when Mama adjusted Aniebie's straps in the living room, and I watched in confusion but laughed each time Mama pushed her shoulders down and warned her about bad posture as a woman. No one was laughing, but my eyes remained downcast and the ones on me felt like they drew crossed lines all over my body as Grandma pushed down my shoulders. The bra beneath my t-shirt pierced my back and the material felt like the burning relaxer Mama applied to my hair. But I didn't dare adjust it or show discomfort. Grandma had taken so much time to make sure it fitted me and the thought of her starting all over again made me keep my back erect. It wasn't just bras and underwear Grandma hand-picked for me at the market; she bought long white socks, new shoes, and what Mama liked to call harmattan season supplies. The supplies usually included face masks, mentholated balms, shea butter, and other body creams. Grandma would look at the product she pulled out of one of the plastic bags, then look around the room before deciding who to give. She'd already looked past me four times before she handed me my masks, balms, and body creams.

'My love, you like them? Your creams are the most expensive.'

Grandma smiled at me revealing her brown teeth and eyes that had numerous smile wrinkles. But as Uduak, Aniebie, and I looked at each other's supplies, I couldn't help but notice I was the only one with different creams. My cream was 'high definition' while Aniebie's was 'moisturising and mild'. The woman on the cover of my cream was pale. On the back side of the pack, one side of her face was dark and the other side *fair & lovely*. Grandma must have noticed my confusion because she spoke to me out of the blue. 'It's not too harsh. It will just make you two shades lighter. You know you have your father's skin tone.'

I couldn't understand why I needed to be two shades lighter. I wondered if Papa was ever told to lighten his shade when he was a boy. I wanted to ask Grandma 'why?' but I asked the heavier question that lay on the tip of my slightly burnt tongue.

'Is there something wrong with my shade now?'

Grandma never faltered to answer questions. She didn't hesitate to tell me why my pee came out with blood when I asked, or why it was important to use sanitary pads. But this time around, grandma asked for water before answering me, and as I watched her take small then large gulps from the glass, I imagined myself two shades lighter. The large family picture that could cover a window aided me. We had taken it the last time Papa came to visit. Mama paid a tailor to sew perfectly-fitted clothes in the same African print and expensive lace materials for all of us. Wearing the same material patterns made my darker skin more obvious.

If I were two shades lighter, I would look just like Aniebie and Mama. My shade would be like Grandma's and perhaps pass for Uduak's radiant tone.

When Grandma emptied the glass, she gave me a smile that didn't show her teeth, and the lines by her eyes that mapped happiness remained flat. I still looked up at her from the carpet hoping for an answer to my question, but Grandma scrunched up her lips as though she wanted to whistle then used them to point at the creams I held. 'Use that one in the morning then the other at night. Okay?'

When I took my shower that night, I used the Fair & Lovely soap and made sure to scrub hard with the tough loofah sponge Uduak helped us pluck from the luffa tree Papa planted in the backyard. My dark skin looked ashy when I used the night cream. I stood in front of the mirror trying to spot a difference in my shade, wondering if I'd be lighter in the two days before the resumption of school. All the while, Aniebie watched me as she conversed with her friends on the phone Papa sent her months ago.

'Don't tell me you plan on using those products Grandma bought for you?' she said, following the pop sound of a sent message.

'Grandma said I should use them,' I replied with a clipped tone as I struggled to clasp the hooks of my new bra, away from Aniebie's wide eyes that ran all over me.

'These are bleaching products, Aniema!'

I'd seen the labels and used Papa's dictionary in the study to check the meaning of the word 'bleach'. But I didn't understand why Aniebie cared, and the familiar ball of anger I felt the day Mama relaxed my hair returned. I bit hard on my bottom lip when she came over to help me clasp the bra. She fiddled with the straps and eased the tension on my shoulders. Our reflections in the mirror highlighted the difference between us in my head again. Just like the family picture did.

'It's not my fault I'm dark.'

Aniebie's thin eyebrows lowered in confusion with an open mouth. 'That's not a fau—'

I shoved her hands off my shoulders. 'You're the one who's Fair & Lovely.'

I got dressed before Uduak called us down for dinner; Aniebie watched me, her light and innocent face conveying shock and disappointment. As I slammed the room door on my way out, I felt the same way about myself. We had never had such an argument. We were always subtle with each other. If we disagreed and it went too far, Uduak settled it by lecturing us on the value of having a sister.

The morning bleaching cream Grandma bought for me made my skin burn when we stood under the harsh harmattan sun for the morning assembly. It made my skin smell like the roasted bulls Mama paid people to kill every Christmas. But just like the relaxer, I was sure the burning meant it was working. Papa had promised to buy me something if I got the first position in class. It was the same thing he said to Aniebie before he bought her a phone. I wasn't just planning on getting the first position, I was also planning on being class captain. It would mean spending more time under the sun while I ran errands from the staffroom to my classroom, but I was determined to show everyone that I was responsible.

The two students who ran against me were new. The new boy always put his hand up to answer questions. He had puffy, big hair and always had something to say. The new girl was often called on by teachers to answer questions. Temi had just moved to Nigeria from England and was just as light-skinned as Aniebie. I felt bad for her each time she was asked a silly question about her parents and when she was coerced to sign up as a candidate for class captain. As our form teacher read out the number of votes for each person, I readied my squeaky new shoes and thought of a place in my room to hang my class captain plaque. But I didn't hear my name the first time, and I was sure that Temi Fasusi sounded very different from Aniema Bassey so it couldn't have been a mistake.

When the teacher called my name, I stood beside Temi as the assistant class captain. I was the one who had spent hours going desk to desk to ask for votes; all Temi had to do was sit and look different. My throat seemed to constrict and my fists balled when she wore the class captain badge, but I got the feeling she was relieved to have me by her side.

We spent most of our time together because of our new positions. I shared my *agbalumos* Grandma brought from the village with her. At lunch, we would spend hours chewing on the fleshy, sour-sweet insides of the fruit until it turned to chewing gum. I taught her how to take quick notes as the teachers dictated and how to be a good class captain who made exceptions for certain noisemakers. Whenever she came over to our house to do some homework together, Grandma complimented her fair skin. She didn't even call Temi by her name. She simply referred to her as my *oyinbo* friend, a term locals used to refer to white people or praise lighter-skinned people. Grandma finally said something about my skin tone one school morning. It was just two months of constant application, and according to her, I was almost a shade lighter. But almost a shade lighter wasn't close to Aniebie or Temi's skin tone. Almost a shade lighter would still make me look different in the family photo.

Mama braided my hair in the living room while I sat on the plush carpet and struggled to keep myself at a convenient reach for her. Each time I thought she was done, she would use the pointed tip of a pen to divide the 'last' part into smaller lines. I didn't have to lean back to feel her tummy. Mama's rounded tummy now hung low when she walked, and she made sure Uduak cleaned the baby's room twice a week. Unlike Aniebie who now loudly prayed about the baby, I still couldn't bring myself to pray about it, and I could hear Mama's early morning prayers downstairs all the way from my room. She often asked God to keep evil and wicked people away from the baby. We still didn't outrightly talk about the baby but the little clothes Mama bought, Mama's visits to the hospital, and Papa's even more frequent phone calls hinted at the excitement we all secretly shared. Thoughts of having a brother came to me more often. I knew he would fit perfectly into the family picture whether he was my shade or Aniebie's, and that thought strangely put a part of me at ease. I didn't want to be the odd girl in the family picture.

Whenever a teacher was done writing notes for the students to copy on the whiteboard, I was called to wipe away the words because of my reach. The eyes I felt on me made me feel like I was trying on a bra for the first time but, this time, in a classroom full of people who scorned me for being friends with someone they liked.

'She's always following Tems' was something I'd gotten used to hearing.

It was easy to know the noisemakers during the silence of a class exercise and steady hiss of the air-conditioner. I wasn't a follower of Temi or Tems, as the other students called her. Anyone who paid attention could see that Temi's hand went up after mine when I excused myself to the toilet and that she used the power of her position to make sure we were in the same workgroup. I got used to the silent remarks that made me chug from my water bottle. On Fridays, I took two water bottles to school. There was something about the last period of the school week that made my classmates bold. It was an intentional free period of silence that was supposed to help us 'reflect on the week'. But Pelumi wasn't trying to be unheard when she mumbled 'Follower of Tems'.

Temi patted my back when I caught an air bubble in my throat from drinking too fast and my back curled from the heavy looks. Pelumi broke away from the undertones of chuckles to a loud 'Follower of Tems.' I held onto my slippery pencil, then put an x before the number twenty beside her name. The sound of the bell sliced through the thick air clouding me. Temi ran off to submit the list of people to be punished on Monday while I made sure the classroom was properly arranged.

'So, I made noise twenty times?'

I could feel over twenty lines stretching across my body while

I stacked rulers. I reached out for my water bottles which usually hung across my shoulder, but there wasn't enough water to push what felt like I'd swallowed a large chunk of meat that refused to go down. Pelumi drew a long hiss that went on and on in my head. The effect it had on me was almost spent, and I had already emptied the content of my second water bottle, when I heard something that made my skin feel like a graph sheet. The word 'blackie' shouldn't have made sense to me. I was almost a shade lighter, thanks to the strict regimen I followed. I could be 'fair & lovely' in nine months if I avoided the sun, and I thought Pelumi understood my struggle. Not because we had been classmates since kindergarten but because we were both darker-skinned. I sucked on the empty bottle hoping that there was some water lodged at the bottom, but the air from it felt thick and teased my throat all the way to my stomach. The hard ball in my throat was just like the one in my tummy, and it was too difficult to suppress this time as I watched Pelumi turn her back to me.

Little stones on the pavement dug into my knees as I knelt outside the principal's office. The usually busy school was empty after closing hours, and one of the compound men moved around with a water hose. I figured he was the one to thank for green grasses in harmattan. I clutched the now broken, jagged-edged wooden ruler until Aniebie gently pulled it from my grasp after letting me drink from her water bottle. Grandma spoke to the principal and told me to write an apology letter to the class for my violent behaviour. Her lips remained upturned throughout the lazy Lagos traffic and through the spicy dinner Uduak prepared. Aniebie and I ate escargots while Grandma made sure Mama ate chicken because she believed escargots make babies dumb and pregnant women sick. Grandma made me explain my actions in the study room after Mama retired to her room. I thought the ball in my throat would resurface, but my words came out with suspicious grace when I said 'they called me blackie.'

Grandma didn't see anything wrong with that, and I gritted my teeth until I couldn't hear a word from her. I wanted her to acknowledge that I wasn't a blackie anymore. All I heard at the end was, 'That's it? Write the apology letter. Good night.' Her bony fingers massaged the sides of her head in frustration before she dismissed me with the flick of her wrist.

I couldn't bring myself to use the night cream, so I sat in the study corner of my room trying to write an apology letter. Aniebie sat on her lower bunk staring at me just like she'd been doing since our argument. I silently longed for her to say something and thought I imagined her usual defiant advice when she said, 'You shouldn't apologise for anything.'

Aniebie examined the contents of the letter over my shoulder with her nose scrunched up before adding, 'It is not a fault to be darker-skinned.' Her smiling eyes had much chatter and stories to tell from the past two months, but before she could settle in the seat beside me to officially resume the *gist*, Uduak opened the door causing the knob to slam into the already indented hole in the brick wall. 'Your mummy is going to the hospital.'

Mama could barely walk down the stairs without her hands on her waist. The night breeze was cold and the driveway covered with dried fallen leaves. Mama gave Aniebie and me tight hugs from the side before leaving for the hospital with Grandma by her side.

The wind felt stronger and the doors sounded like they needed greasing with Mama's absence. I barely ate a thing from the tableful of breakfast Uduak made before Grandma returned and told us to get dressed. Throughout the ride to the hospital, Aniebie's arms were around me, and I could see our translucent reflection through the tinted window, well enough to note our similarities, from the shape of our mouths to the curve of our eyes, and I couldn't help but imagine what my brother looked like.

Grandma shushed us when we entered a room with a *Babies Ward* sign even though we weren't talking. I wondered if it was still too early to talk about the baby and if Mama decided to still give him the name we picked out. Mama gave us the faintest smile; she had a tube connected to her wrist and was on a video call. A baby lay in an open carriage which we quickly surrounded. He only moved a finger from time to time, then offered us a smile that resembled Mama's.

'He looks like me.' My words came easily. Again. Grandma gave the hanging carriage a push before saying 'Yes, she's dark like you.'

Aniebie leaned down, then whispered 'it's a girl' in my ear. My wide eyes followed her pointed finger to the baby's ear lobe that was filled with a thin metal pin earring. The baby let out a small 'aah' that made me want to make sure her clothes were comfortable, and I hoped she didn't feel thin threads across her skin as we stared at her in awe. I ran a finger across the baby's forehead before saying, 'Her name is *Uyai*—Beauty.'

Mama nodded, 'I like it.'

SMALL MERCIES
Henry Mutua

Niko did not tell you that Nairobi was a city of madness. He did not tell you of the desperation that twinkles in the eyes of roadside shoe hawkers who say, 'Which design do you want?' or 'I have Nike and Puma,' or 'at least buy one for the girl.' He did not tell you of the children near the National Archives who sell mint gum and say, 'Nipromote boss tafadhali.' It ripped your heart to see them, these children, faces drawn in hunger and stories you'll never know. And he did not tell you of the pickpockets who bump against your shoulder and reach into your pockets so they can steal your wallet or phone. This you learned when your kabambe phone disappeared as though by a magic trick.

The jacaranda trees were in full bloom and their purple flowers lay scattered on the black tarmac as you waited for Niko. When you were a child, you had seen sights like this in old copies of The Weekend magazine and you had thought that these places—where the light filtered through giant trees in dappled shadows—could only be found in one's imagination. But here you were, a messenger from a dusty village town, with nothing but the Kenyan dream (if ever such a thing existed for people like you) stacked in some dark corner of your mind. Delicate showers fell on the cabro-paved roads along the street where Niko picked you, and in his car filled with Congolese rumba, he narrated how Nairobi was a whole world contracted into one city. You did not understand. You would live with him until you found a place of your own.

He lived in a one-bedroom apartment with his wife and daughter, next to that of a vulgar screaming woman with a lot of children. By his apartment building was a wooden poster: 'Doctor from Zanzibar, Call for job promotion, male virility, love charms.'

His wife looked different, different from the last time you saw her in the village. Her skin looked darker. There were dark circles under her eyes, and she rolled them too often. The last time you saw her in the village was during the Christmas celebrations when she stood at the Church of the Revealed's podium to testify, dressed in a brocade-embroidered gown with a large hand-sewn peacock at the centre. Later, she had led Niko and Pastor Bartholomew to hand out sweets and other assorted gifts like oversized clothes and shoes to street children. Other women in the village (including your gossiping aunts) envied the way her skin looked lighter then. Someone even started selling skin lightening cream, Fair Rose Cream, in the local market—the finger-sized tubs always ran out of stock. Your mama even bought one.

At the table, Niko's daughter said she wanted chips when her mother served cabbage and potatoes. It baffled you that she could choose what to eat. When you were a child, whenever you whined about food, your mama would tell you about those children in Turkana without food. Be grateful for small mercies, she'd say.

When Niko saw your spoon suspended in surprise, he said, 'Children of these days.'

Niko's wife went to the chips vendor downstairs and bought her chips in a clear polythene bag. Cherry-red tomato sauce dripped in the fried pieces like blood. That night, you kept thinking about the wooden poster near the apartment building. *Doctor from Zanzibar, Call for job promotion, Male virility, Love charms.*

Niko did not tell you that you'd work in an oriental restaurant that served delicacies such as Peking Duck and Noodles in Soy Sauce. The name of the restaurant was Mister Cheng's, and the manager was a taut-faced Chinese man with a miniature golden statue of the Buddha on his office desk.

Your work was to wash dishes dripping in soy sauce or cups stuffed with soaked tea bags. You believed you would get food poisoning if you ate anything in that sauce. The Chinese restaurant was among the flurry of expatriate businesses that came with the construction of the Standard Gauge Railway, funded by a Chinese company whose name you couldn't remember. What you remembered, though, was Papa's not-too-original, oft-repeated aphorism: 'Kenyans don't need China's help.'

And you still remembered the Chinese shop owner who insulted President Uhuru Kenyatta, and everyone back at the village turned up at Mama Musee's pub to watch the man being deported on television.

Your country was tumbling back to colonial times like a montage played in reverse, tumbling back to the days when Brits landed in Mombasa aboard ships with regal names like Queen Victoria, with the Union Jack flying atop their masts.

Still, you thought that that racist slur was an isolated incident. A dotted lamb in a pure-white coated flock.

Your partner in scrubbing plates was a Swahili lady, around twenty years old, who said jobs in Saudi Arabia paid better. But didn't you hear (not sure from where) that Kenyans who went to work in Saudi Arabia did things like breastfeed adult men or service their masters? Didn't you also hear that their passports were confiscated the minute they arrived? You once knew a man from your village who travelled to the Emirates and came back with one eye missing, although he had gone to work as a chauffeur, not fight a war. Someone had said that his eye had been sacrificed to the djinns that made those Arabs rich. You knew Arabs were rich because of their oil fields. The Swahili lady—she said her name was Hawa or Hewa—looked at you with her wandering eye, shocked that you knew too much.

She loved saying 'sir' to the Chinese manager, and you despised her for that. For letting her tongue worship someone. She might as well have licked his dark-tanned boots. Every morning, Hawa or Hewa reported to work with puffy bloodshot eyes, and when you asked her, she'd say, 'this Nairobi weather.' You pictured 'this Nairobi weather' as a short plump man who gave too much cold and very little sunshine.

You washed, rinsed, repeated.

Sometimes you stopped to stare at the flowery patterns on the edges of the plates. Other times you traced your fingers on the wicker trays and felt the ridges of the ornate silvered surfaces. You kept a journal of your life in Nairobi. Of the meat in the restaurant's freezer you thought was more than a week old. Of the Mandarin words you were picking little by little as if they were golden pebbles. You wrote it all, giving generously to that leather-covered journal, and it gave back to you in form of solace.

You did not write of the pain that tugged at your heart when you heard the Chinese expatriates say Kenya was number two in corruption in Africa. (Nigeria was number one.) You did not write of the lump that filled your throat and refused to go away when you heard that the restaurant would never serve Africans. You left it all out. You left it out because you thought it would absolve you of that tugging and that lumping. Those blanks were a penance for being a citizen of a country ranked so high in corruption. They expiated you, separated you from the droves of the corrupt ones, and you stayed there. In that little corner where you felt safe.

You always arrived at Niko's house tired and late, and always, you could overhear the vulgar screaming woman next door screaming curses: 'You fool that can't feed your children,' 'Jinga jeuri sana.' One day, you overheard Niko and that woman quarrel about hanging space on the clothesline outside. You went out and met a behemoth of a woman with tightly braided cornrows. She smoked Rooster cigarettes, so her voice was always husky, and on Tuesdays, she fasted for the deliverance of her drinking husband. You would hear her on those days, in the hours before dawn, casting and rendering into the wilderness, asking her children to join her in prayer, lest (she would always add) they took up their father's habit. Later, your mind traced its scent on the memories of her, wondering if the cornrow braids pulled at her temples, whether she could feel any pain on her head.

Niko's wife always had your food in a hot pot, and the couch, your sleeping place, was always readied with a tasselled cushion and a throw blanket.

The day you arrived late at the restaurant—because the traffic jam at the Pangani driveway was bumper to bumper—the Chinese manager had a whip in his hand, his black pupils dilated. You thought it was a joke, him holding a whip. Hawa or Hewa stood close to him like a small girl with her father at the supermarket staring at shelves full of dolls. He tapped the steel worktop with the whip so the whip bounced, and then you said, 'Are you serious?' When none of their expressions changed, you knew he was.

That day, you let the whip land on your buttocks; it was as if you were back in primary school. His lips were pursed, his eyes indifferent as though he were thrashing a wooden post. And yet you held on to that job. You did not write about the whipping;

you left it out.

From that day, you called the Chinese manager, 'Sir.'

Mama and Papa called from the village to check on you. You said you were doing well, and Papa said, 'Thanks to the prayers we say on your behalf.' Mama said you should start sending money for dowry even though you had sent them a thousand shillings the previous week through MPESA. And you hadn't chosen a girl to marry yet.

You were eyeing the Somali girl who sold fabric in the shop next to Niko's house. She smelled of a flowery perfume that made your nose run. You had never spoken to her before. Only the mere 'jambo' when you went to pick new clothes for Niko's wife. You once heard a customer call her Khadijah, and you'd thought the name made your lips tired. If she ever married you, you would have told her to shorten it to Khadi or Dijah or Jah.

On Sundays when you never went to work, you pretended you were buying a newspaper from the vendor outside Khadijah's fabric shop, and as you stood flipping through the pages, you would listen to her voice, a lilting soft dissonance with a Somali accent. You knew the songs she listened to. Mostly Zanzibari bands with virtuosic Nzumaris for instrumentals. You knew she loved to gossip about women who prostituted at Koinange Street and pretended they were holy (even though you never advocated gossiping). You knew she loved her Mahamri with a lot of sugar. All this you knew without talking to her.

The first time you saw her had been during Ramadan, the holy month of fasting for Muslims. She was seated at the shop's entrance, fanning her face with a folded newspaper. Her fingers—they evaded the buibui's cover—were painted a matte black, and you pictured her laughing at your jokes. And yet when you decided to speak with her, your feet froze at the shop's veranda, as if they had been clipped with an axe. Tomorrow was another day, you had said.

The day you collected yourself to go speak with her, Westgate happened. Al-Shabaab gunmen, rumoured to be from the Somali community, stormed the upmarket mall and killed shoppers. Fear *brittled* your bones when you and other workers at Mister Cheng's watched KTN's live coverage of the siege. You remember the anti-Islamic slur in Nairobi that September.

Niko said all Muslims should be dragged by their heads out of Kenya. Niko's wife said not all Muslims were terrorists. A Member of Parliament went on live television to propose a bill that made Christianity the State religion. It did not go past the first reading. The Kenyan police raided Eastleigh, where most Somalis lived, and beat up old men and women, ransacked houses. During a television news bulletin, a bystander with missing teeth said, 'They kept asking where we hid the bomb.'

The next Sunday, Khadijah's shop was different. It hosted a butcher shop with hanging cadavers of cow and goat. It seemed like she had never existed, like she had never been there before. The butcher, an old man with a mole in his chin, said the Somali woman had emigrated, and you realized you were never meant to be together. Perhaps she had never thought of you.

When you saw Khadijah next, her face was plastered on a print edition of *Female* magazine: 'Muslim Women Who Have Escaped Islamophobia in Countries They Served.' You imagined her bundled in a dinghy across the Mediterranean with nothing but hope and the Guardia Civil waiting on the other side. In the magazine picture, she was looking at you, her eyes surrounded by dark mascara, pink rouge on her cheeks. When you held the page against the fluorescent bulb in Niko's sitting room, the picture seemed to move.

Meanwhile, the manager at Mister Cheng's was making you work overtime; the entrance to the restaurant now had a sign, 'No Africans allowed', even though Kenya was against racial segregation.

One day, you saw two African women with Nigerian accents being shoved away even though they drove a humming Range Rover. They were filming with their phones as the bouncers led them away. One of the women was saying, 'We can never go back. We can never go back.'

Hewa was making moves on you. She would roll her buttocks when she walked away from you, and her eyes avoided your gaze when she asked you to pass her the dishwashing gel. You had never taken interest in her wasp-thin waist. Her lips were placed too far apart when she talked, and she painted her nails a beige green. 'Was she an environmentalist?' you thought.

One day, after her leave, she brought you coconuts wrapped in newspaper and said they were from her family's beach plot in Kilifi. The next time she brought you locally brewed coconut beer, and you laughed as you drank at the back of the kitchen. And then the manager found you. There are scars on your hand from trying to shield yourself from the Chinese manager's whips. Hawa was whipped until her skirt gave way at the seams. You remember how funny it was then, her laced underskirt exposed after the whip caught her thighs.

Still, the job was too precious for you to lose, so you held on. Niko asked when you were moving out, and you had no idea. The money was coming, but you were sending most of it home.

And then it happened. The exposé.

The video was grainy, but you would never forget your face. Someone had captured the Chinese manager whipping you. Kenyans on Twitter—those savage online police—wrote things like: 'This should be closed.' 'Did you know they don't serve Africans there?' 'What place is this? The Minister for Interior Security, WTH is this?' 'Send these savages back to China.'

Still, you went to work. Niko spoke to you in a whisper, as though he was afraid in his own home. He told you to keep still; the terror of the Lord would smite your enemies with deadly force. When you went to work, the 'No Africans allowed' sign had been removed, and in its place, a pastel pink had been painted. The bougainvillaea bushes around the restaurant's exterior stood still as if nothing had happened.

A sassy journalist with a chiffon dress accosted you as you entered the kitchen asking questions: 'Do you intend to press charges, Mister . . . what do I call you?' You brushed past her in anger for stabbing at that scar you thought had healed. What was pressing charges for a person like you?

Still, an international human rights organization decided to take your case to court. The organization sent you a letter 'expressing our belief in the core values of humanity'. These core values, they seemed like delicate luxuries, which the organization's lawyers spoke of only in half-glimpses.

You wrote to your parents and lied you were okay even though the restaurant had been closed and you were living on the edge of your toes at Niko's. You didn't disclose that Niko's wife was complaining that the food was getting finished faster. You didn't disclose that Niko's daughter said that the house always smelled when you entered—even after you invested in a Nivea roll-on.

A verdict was reached. The court awarded you five million shillings. The human rights organization would take a portion to represent 'other people like you'. You imagined 'other people like you', voices suffocated by forces beyond their power.

When they got news of the money, Mama and Papa came from the village and crammed into Niko's house. Mama said she saw a vision of a white hand above your head. You never understood.

'Pastor Bartholomew, the one in the village, said you have to be faithful in your tithe,' Mama said.

Papa told you he needed money to repay the loan shark or else he would lose his maize mill machine. You knew there was no loan shark. You knew he would drink all of it. And yet you gave him the money, the amount jotted down in a cheque that smelled of fresh ink.

You even promised to build them a house with a shower on the inside.

Your journal is full, and a local newspaper wants you to comment on issues ranging from 'Liberation of the African people' to the 'Discovery of the Kenyan Dream'.

You opened a restaurant that served things like mukimo and coconut rice and pilau, and at the counter, a girl who looked like Khadijah counted shilling bills and stashed them in the drawer.

Last Saturday at the opening of your Oriental foods menu, you thought you saw Khadijah among the mingling guests who clinked glasses against glasses. You walked up to her, but then you discovered the woman standing before you had broader face features; she didn't have Khadijah's pink rouge, and when she spoke, she lacked a Somali accent.

HUMAN CITIES
Justin Clement

The gods burned, quietly.

Imayinwa watches the man coming down the hill ahead, and the Pull constricts as both their paths converge. She emerges from the cluster of yellowed bluestems into the savannah's shorter grasses, and in a handful of minutes, both cover the distance between them and stand about three feet from each other. Imayinwa says nothing; pleasantries have little meaning. The man says nothing too, and they both stand for seconds, and the late afternoon sun watches them both, until their faces begin to ripple with inquietude.

Imayinwa shakes her head. 'I'm not giving up any.'

'Please,' the man says. He's short, stocky, and his voice has this tinge to it that Imayinwa concludes he is Central African. 'I only have one more left.'

Imayinwa scoffs lightly. 'Don't start.' The man is obviously lying; he is far from the desperation that comes with giving up the last of you, something she has witnessed twice. Imayinwa grimaces; the pain is crossing from simmering to boiling.

The man's face is changing, too. Shades of discomfort swim across his face, and he has begun to bend forward. 'Please,' he says again, and this time, Imayinwa catches the spice of agony underneath.

But it is a pain that mirrors hers, so she shakes her head sharply, then gasps as the pain in her upper abdomen begins to spread red waves of dolour all around her body. As both people sink to the ground, their cries rise in the air. It takes roughly forty seconds for the grunt and screams to be truly earnest, and the fact that of the both of them, it is the man that lets out a true scream first, hardens Imayinwa's resolve, even as she digs her fingers into the thin topsoil, and screams. The man is half lying on his left shoulder before the first words burst out of his mouth. 'When I was a boy—' And immediately, the rising pain in Imayinwa plateaus, then drops, and she turns to her side, panting loudly. The man's breathing is equally laboured, but he continues speaking. '—like seventeen, my mother used to have these chandelier earrings. They were done with white gold, very pretty and expensive. They were her favourite set.' He stops, but he has already begun speaking, so he cannot stop. He goes on. 'One day, I really needed money. It was for a business scheme me and some of my friends in school cooked up. Which seemed like a very good plan at the time.

'So I collected my mother's earrings, and I sold them.' The left side of the man's mouth twitches. 'She had not worn them in a while then, so it took her almost a month to notice that they were not in her drawer anymore. That day, she wanted to wear them to her friend's wedding, and she turned the entire house upside down for them. That was the only time I've seen my mother look . . . wild. She questioned my sister and me, but of course, we both denied seeing them.

'My mother was not herself for more than a week. She stopped making jokes with us, and she barely talked to us except to still ask about the earrings. I did not understand what they meant to her, and why they meant that much. With time, my sister's innocence became clear to my mother, and weeks after, my mother called me aside from time to time and asked me about the earrings. But I continued denying ever knowing about their disappearance. As the months passed, my mother stopped asking me about them.

'She asked me about the earrings again, like five years later. It was one of those conversations that seemed casual, the way she said it with a smile. A pained smile. And I told her I did not know. Years had passed, but I could not carry that guilt that would come from whatever thought or emotion that would sit in her eyes when I told her that I actually took them. So I chose another kind of guilt. I denied it.' The man turns his face from Imayinwa and lifts himself off the ground, looking to his left and blinking rapidly a few times. 'And I kept denying it. For more than thirty years. She asked me about them four other times over the decades, and each time, I looked her in the eye and denied it to her face, even though by that time, we both knew I was responsible. But still, I would deny it. Every time.' The man's eyes return to Imayinwa again, and she notices the crystal sheen to them. 'I denied it till the day she died.'

Silence sits between the two people for three seconds, and the savannah's wind continues to howl lightly. Then the memories begin seeping into Imayinwa.

She sees it, feels it. All of it. The memories unravel in her mind like a morning glory, and with each unfurling petal comes a knowing, an awakening wash of alien memories that will become familiar, that will become her. The memories permeate her understanding; she feels the boyish dogged resolve of the man as a teenage boy as he looks at the delicate earrings in the drawer, before he takes them. Imayinwa feels, and understands, the stubborn cowardice of the man as a young boy, as his mother sat him down on the beige three-seater sofa, asking him about the earrings. Imayinwa experiences the cowardice harden over the years and morph into an equally stubborn guilt which the man—Muhtaram—never let go of, never quite knew how to let go of. The shrouding shame, each time his mother referred to the earrings over the years. Imayinwa sees it all. She feels it all.

When the memory is hers completely, she looks at the man as their contact bond unravels. The Pull grows once more, and both people begin marching forward again. There is no momentary pause when they pass each other. Imayinwa turns to look back after he's walked past though she knows he will not do the same. The memory has been wholly moved from his subconscious to hers, and she watches the man walk through the cluster of bluestems she'd just walked out of, and suddenly, Imayinwa wishes for him to turn again and look at her, just once, out of an irrational impulse to see if he would look and remember. But he does not turn, and after another span of seconds, Imayinwa faces forward, and the sight of the grassland's yellowing expanse greets her again, like a subtly malicious companion.

The first one fell in Lakhdaria, Algeria, onto a bustling street, killing the unfortunate elderly woman who'd not known to leave the coffee shop a few seconds before or after she actually did. When the crowd gathered, it wasn't the woman's death as much as what exactly it was that did kill her that held all of their stares and stretched the limits of what they understood to be reality. The thing was humanoid, its entire skin of a stone-grey colour, and it was significantly bigger than an average person—nine feet in length maybe, with lither, longer limbs. Its face seemed human in structure too, with strong angular definitions, coupled with a hairless head. But its open black eyes had hard, silver irises and miniature vertical slits for pupils. However, the creature, like the body crushed beneath it, was lifeless. This was the first god to fall, and the first of the last Thirteen.

She chose to stop keeping count after one thousand days, but Imayinwa knows she hasn't been walking for up to four years just yet. The sun has just risen, and the sky still wears the blue and orange of mid-dawn. It's been some days since that man, and Imayinwa notes how the savannah's vegetation has thickened over the days; she could be close to a river, or people. She's certain that this far out, any settlement would not have had anyone wealthy enough to have afforded the mutation serum, even from private labs. She'd walked through a village once, months before, and everyone in it had watched in morose silence as she passed briskly. It is one of the most haunting things she's experienced, and still remembers.

Imayinwa blinks and squints at something shadowy moving in the distance. Then, all at once, she feels the resonating oscillation within her, and she curses. Another. She chooses to visualize Wanderers as moving balls that attract each other when close, and then get stuck to each other. But each ball needs to keep moving, and as both balls are being pulled in their respective directions, both are subject to the pain of staying in place. One ball tears away a piece of itself for both to be free and continue along their paths. The detached piece remains on the other. But one ball must give. One ball will give. The thought always strikes Imayinwa as uncannily valid.

This current ball is petite, a seemingly young woman, in a square neck taupe blouse and something that looks like sweatpants. They're still clean, of course; the field around their bodies makes certain of this. The woman and Imayinwa come to a stop before each other, and Imayinwa notices the woman's chin quivers slightly.

'Uh,' the woman says. 'Do you want to . . . talk?'

Imayinwa laughs before she can stop herself, and she is surprised by the genuineness of the laughter. 'That is a good joke. I don't know if you meant it or not.' Her liver is beginning to pulse, a warning.

The woman gives a quick, lopsided smile which disappears as quickly as it appears, and Imayinwa knows that she won't be handing over her memories to this woman—this is a person that really does not like pain. She would cave in first.

The theory holds true, and Imayinwa barely lets out her first guttural cry before the woman quickly starts talking. 'I used to work at this company,' she says. 'And I had this terrible supervisor. We never aligned. He always assigned me the jobs he knew I didn't want, and I think it amused him. I think the fact that I couldn't or I wouldn't do anything about it gave him this impunity. I've never liked making scenes or being the centre of public or even, uh, private attention.

'There was this special office retreat coming up, and he was the one that had to recommend and forward the names of those that merited attendance. And I deserved it far more than anyone in the office. I was being choked by work, by jobs that I didn't like for that matter, and I was being choked by the image of who I was supposed to be, this calm and collected nice woman. But my supervisor did not send my name. And he knew, everyone knew, that I deserved a spot on there, but he didn't include my name. He was literally messing up my life, and he still saw it as amusing. I cried. I cried so much.

'That day of the retreat, I remained in my office, then broke down again. I locked myself in the office, and I was there for what seemed like ages, even past closing hours, but I did not care. I think I came out of my office sometime after eleven that night, and as I walked past his office on my way out, I stopped. I put my hand on the doorknob and pushed down. When the door opened and I stepped into the empty office, at first, I didn't know what to do.

'But,' the woman says, and Imayinwa notices the ghost of a smile at the edge of the woman's lips, 'a really wild idea got into me, and I just closed the door. And I peed all around his office. Everywhere.

On the settees. On the table. All over the carpet. Even on the walls. I had never done something like that in my life, but that day, that day, I felt so good. So . . . alive. It's the only time I can say I've felt free, I guess.' The woman looks into the distance immediately after talking, gives two wistful nods, and then says, 'Yeah.'

Imayinwa absorbs the memory, and they both begin walking forward again, slowly first, then normally. The wisps of Imayinwa's consciousness dance around the edges of her newest bit of self, her memory of a life that belonged to another. Not for the first time, Imayinwa thinks about how her body has become a city filled with foreigners. She thinks it a queer thing, running back to the one place where it's just you, where you're meant to be truly you, and then even there, you're not, still. Surrounded by memories of people that aren't you, and yet feeling like they are yours, are you. Trying to think about your past and instead being drawn into the past of others. What happens when everyone but you has a piece of you? Do you still exist?

> 'Experiments . . . show that the DNA of the creatures falling out of our atmosphere is . . . similar to ours . . . But some talk within the scientific community . . . indicate . . . that extraction of the bizarre gene, now termed Delta-Q, and its introduction into human DNA . . . cell division could carry on exponentially. Maybe even infinitely.'
> —Culled from Dr Isaac K. Ajayi's interview in The New Quantum Review, 601.

She isn't sure why exactly she gives it up, but she does so anyway. Imayinwa grunts through the pain before speaking. 'When my sister and I were young girls, we did not get along much. Then, there was this day that we had this fight and then she came in when I was drawing and said something that really, really angered me, and—I couldn't stop myself—I turned around and drove the biro I was holding into her right eye. That moment was unreal.

'It was like everything around me grew quiet for a very tiny fraction of time, and then it was followed by the sound of my sister shrieking. That is the most horrific moment of my life. That was the day I was branded the black sheep of my entire family, even up to my extended family. The girl who stabbed her own sister's eye. That was the day the relationship between me and my sister was permanently defined; we would never have a close relationship on this earth or in this life.

'But the thing that strikes me most about that day is that underneath it all, I wasn't sorry I did it.' Imayinwa blinks slowly, twice, and keeps her eyes distant. 'I'm not sorry I did it.' She exhales. 'My sister has worn eye patches for years because of me, and I am still not sorry.'

The memories begin to disentangle from Imayinwa's mind in trailing, wispy pieces. Pockets of the events fade to oblivion in her mind, and she doesn't try to grasp onto them this time, unlike in the beginning. It is a futile thing. Soon, she forgets it all, and her body jerks forward, and she begins moving forward again.

There is a memory she can no longer remember now; the bearer she cannot remember too, and she realizes, as she walks, that she has given up an Intimate. She hopes the person was worth it. She thinks the person must have been.

'The United Kingdom has successfully synthesized the world's first mutation serum from the falling creatures, with a mutative potency of 99.76% . . . A new era for mankind . . . Homo sapiens can now touch infinity and become a new species. Homo immortales.'
—Culled from an article in Blue Polygon, December 2029.

* * *

There isn't much of her left to give, so Imayinwa has decided that this tall, bald man with skin like mahogany must give up the Intimate.

'This is my last memory,' he says, and under different circumstances, Imayinwa would have liked to hear him sing.

'I don't care,' she tells him instead.

Their agony session is fairly long, a minute thereabout, and Imayinwa bites her bottom lip so hard that she breaks the skin momentarily, before it rapidly heals and leaves her front teeth stained with blood.

Then through his cries, the man shouts, 'I grew up in poverty!' The pain plateaus in Imayinwa, recedes, and the man starts to speak, in a straight, oddly distant tone. 'We were not poor to the point of living on the streets, but it was to the point that my siblings and I became enemies when it was time for food. My father would usually serve our food on one plate and set it before the six of us. So we would fight and grab and eat what we could reach.

'Everything was a struggle. We struggled with school fees. We struggled with house rent. We struggled with proper clothes. Even before my father put the importance of earning money into my head, life taught me directly that earning money is important on this Earth. My father would always tell me to study hard, to read and pass my exams well. That I should read a good course in the university so that I could secure a good job.' He makes a sound that seems part laugh, part scoff. 'He didn't know how to explain to me the point of all my reading if we could not even afford my acceptance fee, not to talk of my school fees. I couldn't get into the university after secondary school, so I had to hustle. I had to work hard. In all ways, good and bad.

'With time, I made headway in my life, and then finally, the day came when I was to receive my first million cedis. One-point-four-six million cedis. My first million, born of my sweat.

'When that money dropped into my account, and I saw those two commas, that was the moment everything about my life changed. That text message, that credit SMS, signified many things about my life. It was like I could breathe properly, for the first time. Over the years, I made much more money, but that first million cedis was the beginning of it all. It was the true symbol of . . . of my transition from poverty.'

When Imayinwa absorbs the memory completely, to her mild shock, the man's irises begin to glow, bright silver, until they become white rings around his pupils. His fingertips begin to fade away first, and then his arms and his feet too, and the man slowly sinks to the ground as the visible flesh outside his clothes disappears. The man turns his eyes toward Imayinwa as he is erased, and in seconds, he is no more, and all that remains of the soul that was are the green cotton shirt and brown corduroy pants on the grass. It was his last. This is the third time she is taking someone's final memory, but she still doesn't know whether this thing, this strange sibling of death, is a good or a bad thing.

'Private laboratories continue to crash global governments' prices. The Delta-Q mutation serum hits six figures for the first time in almost nine years.'
—Culled from the headline of The Tower, May 13, 2038.

When Imayinwa makes out the woman's face clearly, something unsettles within her, and she does not understand what it is, or why it unsettles her. As they get closer to meeting, Imayinwa notices the woman's fair skin and wide lips and the way her flowing vermillion djellaba moves through the surrounding air. Moroccan, maybe? They get to each other, and both women stop walking. A few loose strands of hair on the woman's head dance in the breeze, and she breathes in deeply, shakily, just before a dark resolve appears in her eyes, which makes Imayinwa's heart beat a little faster.

This is a person like her—having so little of themselves left to hold on to, they hold the little, with everything.

Both say nothing, and soon the woman places her right hand on her upper abdomen, seconds before Imayinwa does. Imayinwa grits her teeth and tries to count the seconds, even as their pain augments. Twenty seconds have them clutching their abdomens tightly. Thirty-three has the woman cry out. Soon, Imayinwa is aware of the vastness of a single second, as more nerve cells in her body begin to register lucid pain. The woman's knees drop to the grass before she lets out a splitting scream. Two seconds later, Imayinwa bends forward and topples to the ground as her scream breaks through. Soon, both women are crying, writhing, and screaming at the top of their voices.

Tears are leaving Imayinwa's eyes, and in her body's paroxysms, she involuntarily twists, and her barely open eyes momentarily rest on the woman's form. It is now Imayinwa sees that the woman has turned her face, through the torment, to look at her. Even as Imayinwa closes her eyes and screams again, her eyelids part to reveal the woman dragging her left arm across the dry grass and doing something. A gesture. The woman's fingers are contorting, bending through the pain, and her index is trying to form something. Then another scream tears out of the woman's lips, and she raises the arm as she turns, trying her best to maintain the gesture, and it is now Imayinwa understands.

One.

An Intimate that can make this woman beg, not to end the pain but to keep her memories, is something Imayinwa somehow accepts to let her hold onto for a little while longer. Imayinwa makes the choice now, to become exactly like the woman. 'I had true friendship once!' Both women gasp as the pain subsides.

Imayinwa draws her lips tightly together. 'There was this particular time I was going back to school, and there was this girl that sat beside me on the flight. Something happened, and we got talking during the journey. Lagos to Port Harcourt isn't a long flight, so there was little time to talk, but we had plenty to say.

'It was new to me, talking to someone like that, because I'm someone with terrible social skills. We talked about serious stuff; we made jokes and all. It was like . . . natural. Like we had been friends for years. When we got to Port Harcourt, we exchanged contacts. But after that day, I never got that call from her. I tried her number for days, for weeks, but it never went through, always unavailable. Then after a while, my phone got bad, and I couldn't get it fixed. That's how I lost touch with someone that filled a space in me that I didn't know existed. It was good. It felt weightless. I felt weightless. Weightlessly happy. Even if it was only for an hour or so of my life. I wondered what happened, wondered if her phone went bad or got stolen or something. But in ways, I cherish that moment because it was true, and the fact that it happened just once shows that it was good. It was too good to last more than it did. And it's what makes me believe and appreciate that moment. For that space of time, I finally had something like a best friend.'

Imayinwa cries. Not the body-wracking type, but the quiet, gasping kind, as the memory is pulled apart, dissolved, and removed from her mind. She stops crying when the memory is gone, and she gets up and begins to walk once again. The tears mark her face for some minutes more, and then they, too, like the memories, fade away.

'I can't stop, I can't stop moving! Help me! Help me, please!'
—Words of Jeremy Mathers, the first immortal to Wander, caught on video.

* * *

The person in the dainty lilac sundress standing before Imayinwa tonight couldn't have been more than twenty when she was administered the mutation serum, and before Imayinwa can stop herself, she asks, 'How old were you before this?'

The girl blinks, then narrows her eyes at Imayinwa briefly, before answering, 'Twenty-one.'

'Oh.' She was more than twenty.

When Imayinwa doesn't seem to be giving up a memory after the first eleven seconds of pain, the girl doesn't allow her torture continue long. 'My mum died when I was a little girl. The last time I talked to her, we all went to the hospital. She was . . . wasting away. Withered down to her bones. The hospital room smelled really bad. And I knew that she was the one that smelled like that. As she was on that bed, she asked me what I wanted. And I said I wanted cookies. Chocolate cookies. My mother was dying.' Hardness had entered her voice. 'And all I wanted at that moment were chocolate chip cookies. And you know what? She had them order it anyway. I was young, I know, but still, I could have said other things, you know. I should have said something else. I could've said I wanted her to get better. But I didn't. Instead, I wanted fucking cookies.' The young girl sniffles, and her eyes shift between anger and a harrowing anguish. 'That was the last conversation I ever had with my mother.'

When they are both untethered from each other, Imayinwa looks into the distance, into the dark blue horizon of the late night, and she nurses the memory with a certain sort of tenderness, and she is glad, and honoured, to be the one embodying the memories of the greatest regret of Cecilia's life. Imayinwa looks back again, and she watches the girl, far-off, walking deeper into the savannah as the night winds play with her hair and sundress from multiple angles. Imayinwa opens her mouth to yell out the girl's name, but the futility of it, regardless of the outcome, registers in her mind, and the yell comes out as a wispy *hey* which the wind holds and takes away.

Was it death that people feared, or was it simply oblivion?

> '*The humans who have altered themselves seem to be attracted by a force or purpose; a command so beyond mortal comprehension that their carbon-type bodies can only translate it into one action: walk.*'
> — Maora, of the Nååri.

This man's newest memory haunts him. It's his first time with someone's final memory, and he does not know what to . . . *be*. Even before the woman let the memories go, the spectres that hid behind her eyes, the earmarks of the dark world that lay behind those windows, would have stuck with him.

The woman had two lives, once. The second was revealed on a Sunday morning, in front of the bathroom mirror, with a strip in her right hand. He wasn't quite a partner, the father. More like a sex buddy. Or exactly like a sex buddy. The staggering, stunning nature of the whole situation left her half-dazed for most of the day. In that daze did she decide out of the blue to go with the family to church, despite not setting foot in any kind of religious concept, physical or mental, in almost a decade. It happened to be the first time in a while that all family members were present at the same time, shocking even more that they were all in church on a Sunday. After the church service, the woman's father pushed for a family photo, and everyone thought it a nice idea. The woman hadn't thought so but the thought of raising an issue, of being seen as the one trying to ruin a possible family photograph, was more weight to her burdened mind, and so she said nothing.

The final photo that they all seemed to like, the woman included, to her tempered surprise, was one in which her mother and father stood in the centre, holding hands, while she stood by the left, her mother's right side, and her younger sister, wearing a yellow-orange ankara eye patch, stood on the right of the picture, by their father. The woman's right hand is lightly, unconsciously, pressed against her belly, seemingly showing off for the camera the silver ring on her index finger, with her black sweater as a backdrop. The man understands how the woman is aware that she is the only one that knows that there are five members of the family in the photograph.

Through the woman, he understands invisibility, the primary ingredient of all secrets, and his mind shows the woman, always keeping that picture close, long after she'd stopped her child at the door and sent her to where all lives end up. One memory sears his mind, and it is the one of the woman crying and bleeding in the bathtub in her apartment, a day after the second pill, thinking of how she spilt the blood of what would have been her child even before she knew her. She wanted a her. She would have loved a her. But just not then. Not then. That picture is the woman's most important relic of what it means to be family. And it is the closest thing to capturing the truest knowledge of her life, a dark truth Imayinwa came to see and accept much too early in life.

She was the one who was never compatible with true happiness, that one who would always ruin the good things chanced enough to find her.

The man raises his gaze to the rising moon in the distance. Translucent, it seems like an alien god of glowing silver, slowly travelling across the violet sky, and the man stares at it, as he continues, walking.

THE DISTANCE IN-BETWEEN
Dennis Mugaa

And so as they sat at Rockefeller Center's sunken plaza, with the Statue of Prometheus shimmering in gold, Wangarĩ said to Michael, 'You know Kenya's flag will be up there soon.' She pointed to the different flags fluttering in the breeze around the plaza. 'I saw the flag on the news. It has stripes of black, white, red and green, and a shield and spears in the middle. Can you imagine the colonial government has the nerve to say they are giving us independence? We fought for it!' The waiter served them their food, and Michael sunk into his plate. Wangarĩ barely touched hers but rather proceeded to talk about Timau, where she had grown up. She didn't talk about it much, and neither did he ask as often.

Michael looked up from his plate and saw her, really saw her. She wore a velvet dress with a grey brooch. Her mouth formed lines, excited lines, the kind he had seen when they first met. She talked about the rivers where she used to play with her half-brothers and sisters, the rolling hills where they used to run and hide, and how once she had nursed a freedom fighter back to health after he had been wounded. He didn't believe her on the latter, but there was an honest way her eyes lit up that made him inclined to accept it as absolute truth. And he wanted to know more; he wanted to know everything, to meet her where her words were, to live in them, in a past he felt distanced from.

'Wangarī,' he said. His legs shuffled beneath the table and he wondered whether he was going to do it. Sunlight dripped down her skin like brown chocolate melting on tongue. As she spoke, he realized she never changed her accent like other immigrants he met, even when waiters said they couldn't understand her when she asked for water. She was different. She was self-contained in a way no other girl he knew was. Now, the moment was perfect. The second-hand ring he had obtained from an old dilapidated antique store suddenly felt heavy in his pocket, burning and drifting around as though it had acquired a life of its own. For two weeks, he had carried it, and yet whenever he saw her, he faltered. Hadn't they been together for the last three years? Hadn't she said that he was— not Columbia University, not the Mboya Airlift programme—the best thing to have happened to her? And she had met his mother, and his mother had loved her. Why then had he hesitated for so long?

Perhaps it was because she had told him a month ago that she was leaving for Nairobi. She announced to him she had been hired in the Ministry of Foreign Affairs. At first, he didn't understand; he thought after their graduation she would look for a job in New York. After all, she had told him her scholarship money would cease at the end of summer. When he understood, he was angry at her, and they argued violently. He feared losing her, but he didn't want to seem desperate or insecure. And so he said he was happy for her although he felt deeply wounded. She said they would still be together, a long-distance relationship could work; she trusted him, did he trust her? She would save and visit him when she could. They would write letters. But he knew that no amount of words could express his passion, his desire, his longing for her. And even if she scented her letters, as she said she would, they would arrive with the scent faded. But what if they were married?

'I'm glad you asked me to come for The March tomorrow. I'm so excited!' Wangarĩ said.

He felt she was sincere. She understood African American history deeply. She knew about the civil rights movement: the student sit-ins, the bus boycotts, and the protests ongoing in the country. She could explain how Jim Crow laws in the South led to the Great Northward Migration. She was the first person to tell him that slaves committed suicide by jumping overboard from ships in the Middle Passage. It was a history that explained his identity, his sensibility, and his politics: it greatly mattered to him. However, the truth was, he had only asked her to The March because he couldn't endure spending an entire day without her.

'Wangarĩ—'

He ran his fingers across his forehead, hoping he had imagined the drip of sweat. She picked up her fork and dug into her plate. He stared at her. It felt like he had been waiting forever for her to finish speaking. 'What?' she asked, in between a mouthful of food. And still, he lingered, unsure of what to do, gazing at her as her cheeks flushed and she put a hand across her face. He fumbled in his pocket and felt for the ring, flaming as he was.

'I want to show you something,' Wangarĩ cried, and his heart dropped.

She fished out a letter folded at irregular angles from her bag. The top part was crumpled, and it was clear that she had read it several times. She smoothed it out.

'It's from my mother. She must have asked the priest to write it for her.'

> *Dear Wangarĩ, I hope that you are doing well. Why don't you write more? We are all glad that you have finished school and you are coming back. Mwenda is much older now, he asks about you all the time. I have told him that you will come back with the plane from America. We*

are all waiting for you and I pray that God blesses you
on your way back. You have been away for far too long.

The letter went on and on. He heard her voice tremble as she read it. He imagined the words crossing the Atlantic in a slow, methodical way and lighting up in flames when they reached her, pulling her away from him.

He couldn't hold back any longer.

'Wangarī, I want you to marry me. Please say yes.' He had planned the proposal for so long, but when the question tumbled out of him, it felt hurried, disordered, and more out of jealousy than anything else. The only comfort, he felt, was that at least his voice sounded sincere. She became silent, her eyes bulged, and she leaned back slightly. 'I wanna be with you forever.' He held out the ring, and when it didn't glimmer in the sun, he wished he had sold everything he owned for a Tiffany.

'Oh, Michael.' She paused. 'I don't know what to say. I don't know what to say.' Time froze, as though everything was happening beyond him, without control. 'I have to think about this Michael. It's too much. You know I'm leaving in two days. It's too much.'

His composure wavered: she hadn't said yes or no. 'No, it's okay. We can get married when you get back.'

'Michael, I've told you I don't know when I'll come back. I haven't seen my mum, my family, and my friends in four years. There's my new job. I'm needed at home. I want to be home for some time.' She averted her eyes from him, and he felt as if something irrevocable had happened. 'I'll save up and come,' she said finally, without conviction.

'When people leave, they forget,' he said, his voice crackling through to fill the resulting silence.

'How can I forget you? Things will be the same.'

'They won't be the same.' His hands held onto the table in desperation as if he were also holding onto her words. 'It's your fault they ain't gonna be. You are leaving.'

'No, Michael it's not that simple. If you truly want to be my husband, why don't you come with me?'

He always found himself unprepared for arguments with her, which was why he said the first thing that came to his mind: 'I can't leave New York, but we can live here, together. Ma is all on her own after Dad died, and our friends are here—'

'Your friends, Michael! Your Mother! Your life!' She turned away from him again and looked out at a nearby fountain. The more she remained silent, the more absurd his words sounded. 'Tomorrow, okay? We'll talk about this on the way to The March,' she said.

He felt a profound loneliness as they walked down Fifth Avenue. He longed for her as they waited for the train together, as they tore and bit into each other inside her Harlem apartment, as music filled the entire house with passion, as he failed to set the alarm clock, and as he wallowed in her lavender scent that also smelt of white-water lilies, for all those future moments he thought he had but now felt were passing him by.

The train ground to a halt at the 49th Street Station. Wangarī sprang up from her seat, disregarding Michael. His face seemed to implore her to sit down and wait, but they did not have the time, and it was his fault they had missed their charter bus to The March.

The doors slid open, and she squeezed her way through a throng of people. The heavy stale air of the station seeped into her skin and made her feel sick. She had never gotten used to subway stations: perhaps it was the clattering of hundreds of feet, or the homeless people lying on carton boards, or the anxiety she felt standing behind the yellow line waiting for a train. What was odd, however, was that she liked tunnels and the feeling of a train moving through the tracks and her surrendering to the sound of metal softly clashing against metal and then emerging in a different place.

'Hold the door!' a man in front of her shouted. He lumbered forward towards the train in breathless haste as it was about to pull out and disappear into the distance.

Wangarī was past the turnstile when she felt Michael straggling behind her. She pulled away when he tried to hold her hand. 'Wangarī, wait!' he called out. She ignored him and started climbing the stairs that led out of the station. The walls were aswirl with graffiti, and even though she didn't like the patterns drawn, it was one of the things she would miss about New York: a form of ordered chaos both frightening and exhilarating.

'Wangarī, wait, this is the wrong station!' Michael screamed. 'It's cold outside.' He removed his jacket and handed it to her. She rejected it, shot him a cold glare, and continued walking up.

Cold morning New York air encircled her like a storm.

It was raining and the tarmac had turned dark. The rain smelt grey and musty. She unfurled her umbrella and finally slowed down to wait for Michael. They walked across the pedestrian crossing in silence. Although she was angry that he had forgotten to set the alarm clock, she was also secretly pleased because it meant they wouldn't discuss his proposal.

Late summer in Times Square felt cold, hurried, and impersonal: cars hooted, yellow cabs stopped at what seemed to be the wrong spots, three men unloaded boxes from a truck outside Hotel Edison, and various advertisements exploded in a kaleidoscope of colour despite the grey of the rain. A billboard announced the showing of *Cleopatra*; Michael had taken her to see it the week before and she hadn't been able to hide her disapproval. She had read Cheikh Anta Diop's work on ancient Egypt, and she knew the characters could not all have been Caucasian. When she scoffed sardonically in the middle of a silent scene, people turned to look at her, including Michael, who she thought would understand. 'Et tu, Michael?' she wanted to ask but was hushed by a passing usher.

Around her, people walked in a rush while others tried to shield themselves from the rain under the eaves of buildings. New York roared on, oblivious of her imminent departure, as though she only belonged to it for a time, but it didn't belong to her. She began to feel from Michael the consequence of her leaving. She had avoided seeing it, but now the profound loss in his eyes made her falter, and for a moment, she was not sure if she wanted to leave.

'Look at that,' she said as she stopped, mesmerized. She momentarily forgot their rush as her anger fell an octave lower. It was always this way with her and jazz music: it made her pause. In a corner of the street, beneath an American flag, a man was playing the trumpet. His cheeks enlarged as he blew into it. Beads of rainwater flowed down his skin, soaking his clothes. Beside him was a 'Freedom Now' poster. His fingers danced in enchantment. He gave them a look of solidarity, half smiling, and then he closed his eyes to let the music flow. It streamed out of him like the rain, rising and falling to the sounds of the city. The tune he played was a rendition of a song she could not quite place.

She turned to Michael. He was less anxious now, humming along to the tune in that nonchalant way of his. It was natural that Michael knew it. Michael who knew every song that had ever been sung and would ever be sung. Michael who told her about jazz clubs in the French Quarter of New Orleans where the sound was first perfected. He had introduced her to Harry Belafonte, Ray Charles, Louis Armstrong, and Nina Simone, and her life had not been the same since. She had bought an old gramophone and jazz tunes filled her apartment, and when she closed her eyes and moved with the music, it felt like she was dancing in purple rain.

'We got to move,' Michael said as he dropped a dollar bill into the man's hat. He held her hand, and this time, she didn't resist. He led her towards the Port Authority where they hoped to find an interstate bus to The March. They moved as quickly as the rain and umbrella allowed.

The March was the culmination of years of struggle for civil rights. While its importance to Michael went unstated, for her it was a way of experiencing the fight for rights and freedom; she equated it to the fight for independence in Kenya. She often drew parallels between her life and Michael's. Michael grew up in the projects in Harlem, she in the native reserves after her family's land was seized and given to white settlers. Michael was denied entry into white-only colleges, she was denied admission into a white-only high school. Michael read poets and writers of the Harlem Renaissance, she read Négritude poets and writers. She believed in Pan-Africanism, believed that all black people shared a common destiny. And yet, when she envisioned an independent Kenya, she felt it was where she should be.

But was she really going to leave? She loved Michael, and somewhere in the middle of the night, that love woke her up, and she almost tore up her plane ticket. She loved him because she saw herself in him. She had found New York through his eyes: the bench he sat on in Central Park during winter to marvel at skating rinks, the best restaurants which served Negroes, the Nation of Islam mosque near his apartment, the music store in Lenox Avenue which had saved him from Harlem streets when he was a rage-filled teen, and the library on 124th Street where he swore he had read more books than any white man alive. He meant the world to her, a separate world, but one she possessed nonetheless. However, regardless of how much Michael created a way of being for her, she knew there were places he could never reach. He could never understand her feeling of dislocation: her longing when she read her mother's letters, her nostalgia for the rivers she swam in, and her excitement at being part of a new nation. By proposing, he upset a balance. He dropped her in the middle of the sea, between two shores: him, where her love was, and home, where her heart was. These thoughts mingled and intertwined so that she no longer noticed the buildings or the people they passed except Michael in front of her who acted as all men in love: desirous of her and everything else at the same time.

'We almost there.' His voice pulled her back from within herself. Before them, several people formed queues outside Greyhound buses marked 'Washington Monument Express'. The rain had subsided, and most of the crowd chose to brave it rather than lose their seats. She wondered how they would get any bus at this point. For a moment, she considered walking to D.C. but remembered her friend Sharleen had started walking there twelve days before with CORE members.

Michael craned his neck and surveyed the buses. He knew this was the biggest march in the country, but somehow he hoped that someone had chosen to miss their bus. He went to the ticket counter. 'Sorry sir, there are no more tickets to Washington.' In desperation, he led her through the crowd, all the way to the windows of bus drivers immersed in *The New York Times*. 'Are there seats available?' he asked each of them. Most shook their heads; some did not even turn to look at him.

By the time they reached the end of the line, his legs were tired and wobbly, his heart was heavy with a wrenching feeling that, for the second day in a row, he had missed out on something he had been looking forward to. They went and stood beside a wall. Wangari swept an arm through her hair. She had trimmed it, but it still formed kinky curls at the ends. Michael rested his palms on his knees. Wangari started pacing about, and he wondered what she was thinking. 'I am sorry,' he wanted to say, but the words wouldn't come out.

'There! Look!' Michael yelled as his eyes shone with renewed hope. They wove their way through the crowd, brushing against bodies that buzzed with warmth and enthusiasm. 'Marlon! Marlon!' he shouted and waved. From across the horde of people, Wangari saw the slender figure of Marlon. He was ushering people into a charter bus. He was one of Michael's closest friends from the NAACP. She had never liked him, but at that moment, his presence felt like a saving grace.

'Michael, whatchu doing here. Shouldn't you be in D.C. by now?' he cried. Michael hesitated and looked down.

'We were left by the bus; it was my fault,' Wangarī said.

'I know it was his, a brother can't keep time for nothing.' He burst out laughing and nudged Michael's shoulder. 'Com'on, get in, the bus ain't full.' Michael, almost in tears, gave Marlon a warm appreciative hug.

They found empty seats at the back, and Wangarī sat down next to the window. Marlon entered last, and the bus dropped into gear.

The rain faded into the clouds, and the day began to brighten. Behind them, the Empire State Building disappeared into a dwindling skyline. She regretted that in all her time there, she had never been to the observation deck. That was New York to her, fading like an old memory. She held Michael's hand, and he smiled at her, and it hurt her to see that his smile held not just the hope he had for The March but also the hope he held for the two of them.

She woke up to clapping and the smell of the sea. She was surprised to find that she had slept through a major part of the journey, but even more so that Michael had not moved his chest from where she laid her head. She felt his chest labour to rise and fall and his heart start to beat faster and faster, as though he were afraid of all things at once. She felt his warmth too, and knew she would sleep with him that night. It would confuse him and confuse her more, but at least they wouldn't talk. It never helped talking about precarious issues.

Outside the window, the port of Baltimore raged on. A large ship was docking and white smoke rose out of it into a clear sky imitating a low hanging spiral cloud. The clapping grew louder as the bus swept through the road approaching Washington. The driver joined in the gaiety, snapping his fingers and making a windmill motion with his hands.

When she lifted her head, Michael mumbled something into her ear which she did not hear at first. 'I told you The March will be peaceful, they said it wasn't gonna be.' She sat up and tried to take in the atmosphere, blend in and feel like she was part of it all. But her demeanour was stale, contrasting his in every way. Marlon must have noticed because he started walking down the bus aisle. When he reached the back, he rested an arm across the seats in front of them and stared at her with a distasteful grin.

'Com'on Waaangarī,' Marlon said. She hated the way he said her name. 'You two are gettin' married, be happy.'

She locked eyes with Michael, and his skirted awkwardly away from hers. She knew Marlon never bothered to read social cues and that he harboured a morbid fascination for the affairs of others. The longer he stood there, the more uncomfortable she felt. Then the driver called his attention, and as he went to the front of the bus, Wangarī felt like she could finally breathe. Cars beside them waved banners proclaiming 'Jobs and Freedom'. The windows in the bus flew open and almost everyone jutted their heads outside to wave at hooting drivers and shouting pedestrians.

'Com'on, lemme see your ring,' Marlon said as he floated back to where they were seated. She turned her head. The gloom Marlon brought with him had returned. Michael shifted in his seat, speechless. She half-heartedly pulled out her hand and stretched it out before him. There was no ring on her finger.

'What! Are you joking?' he asked, the tone of his voice rising. She hoped Marlon would let them be. Instead, he turned to Michael. 'You didn't ask?'

'We're working on it Marlon; she's got to go home first,' Michael said at last.

'Back to Africa, huh?' He leaned in closer to them, as though he wanted to be sure, swallowing the space between them. 'You know, one day I'll come to the motherland. We ain't in America willingly, you know. We are here because *you* sold us.'

She felt hate rise inside her, from her stomach to her throat, churning like bile. She wanted to tell him that what he was fighting for meant nothing if all he could do was ascribe blame. They were on the same side. She wanted to insult him but slumped back into her seat and felt something inside her capitulate.

Marlon left and Michael turned to her. 'I'll come with you.'

'Michael, not now.' She turned away from him. He looked at her. She felt him looking, but she looked out of the window. She saw herself embracing her mother for the first time in four years; she was playing with her brothers and sisters in Timau; and she was working in the new government's office in Nairobi. All the things that did not include Michael. What was this forever he wanted? Didn't it mean the rest of her life? Shelving her past for a future that entailed him, and only him.

'I'm serious, I'll come with you,' Michael said as he fished a photograph from his jacket. 'Once I finish law school, I'll come right away. Here, have this.' The photograph showed the two of them smiling at the steps of Low Memorial Library in their graduation gowns. She remembered Michael's mother crying at the sight, proud and in disbelief, and she wished that her mother could have been there too.

'No, you keep it. It's yours.'

'I want you to have it, show your mother.' She took it from him as the excitement in the bus rose to a crescendo.

'We have reached; this is history we are making; everyone will remember this day!' the driver boomed as he swung the wheel left.

The bus drifted into Washington, and the capital unfolded out to her like something from a history book. The streets were crowded. Buses and cars were parked beside them; some moved slowly ahead of them winding along as far as her eyes could see; it seemed as though the entire country was present. People had come from Georgia, from Alabama, from Mississippi, and other states she could not name. The sun shone in a glorious yellow; there wasn't a single cloud in the sky. The driver brought the bus to a complete stop as there was no room ahead. They alighted and prepared to walk the remaining distance.

They were met by the largest crowd of people Michael had ever seen. And they had gotten there late—late! He could smell change in the air, oozing from the buzzing crowd, their faces gleaming and sweltering in the heat. Most of them had 'March on Washington' buttons or banners—Black, White, Hispanic, their arms locked in solidarity as they marched past the Washington Monument singing 'We Shall Overcome'. It was possible that things could change, that they could be different. And yet, when he looked at Wangarī as she smiled at him, his heart sank.

'I can't believe it! All these people! This is it! This is how things change!'

'You will write to me?' Wangarī asked him. It wasn't a question or a statement; it felt like it was something she ought to say, though perhaps a day too early.

'Yes, yes, every single day.'

'Quiet, Martin is speaking,' someone said.

Her face glowed in the afternoon sun and held him in an enchantment he couldn't explain. And then, she wasn't there anymore.

She was ahead of him again. She was walking past the reflecting pool where people had dipped their feet to cool, and he struggled to find his way through. 'I have a dream . . .' he heard from the speakers, and the atmosphere became electric. People cried and waved their arms. Those perched on trees were in euphoria. It was more than he could have imagined. 'Wangarī.' But she didn't turn. She also didn't turn when he said goodbye to her at the airport, and neither did she respond to every letter he wrote but never mailed. She flamed away from him like a dream in morning light.

REMEMBER ME
Chidera Nwume

Who are you behind closed doors?

A common question with different connotations, depending on the context of the conversation. Pastors use it to remind their congregation that though they can pretend to others, there is an Almighty who sees them. It is a chilling reminder that secret doings do not go unnoticed. God sees all. Potential lovers bring it up coyly in conversations. 'Who are you behind closed doors?' becomes 'what can you do when the lights are turned off?' Who do you become when you two are alone, with nothing between you but the heat of lust and longing? What can you do in bed?

Today you sit alone on yours and ask yourself this question, but you are neither a chastising pastor nor an aroused lover. You are a pensive final year student wearing your father's red T-shirt that grazes your mid-thigh when you stand, probing yourself because, truly, you do not know, or maybe you do, but you are coming to terms with your true self, the real you, that nobody, including you, was aware of before now. The truth is that you don't know who you are, but you've always believed that one could never know oneself fully. It's the same way you are not sure of how you look. You stand in front of the mirror before leaving the house, long enough to be sure that you look okay, but not enough to notice the flaws you are so fixated on; otherwise, you would never leave. The days you do notice them, you cry and cover your mirror with a dirty pillowcase for days. You don't understand how your mother and friends can call you beautiful. Where is the beauty? In your B cup breasts with angry red spots all over them or in your belly squeezed by your waist beads? You know these people cannot all be lying to you, but you also cannot connect the two, so you are left in this confusing middle ground. Tabs on body dysmorphia lay open on your Safari app, but you never get around to reading the WebMD answers. You're not sure you should.

There are a few things you are sure of, however. You know your name, Ayemere—'I will be remembered'—a depiction of the kind of life your parents hoped you would live. You imagine that your father had said this in a solid tone when he looked down at your squirming body fresh from your mother. 'Yes, my daughter will be remembered!' And your mum would have nodded wearily. Or maybe it was more for him; he has always been a proud man. Maybe he meant that you would be his legacy, that because of you, he would be remembered, considering the eight years spent waiting and praying for a child. 'I will be remembered.' You know you had not turned out as assertive as he would have liked. In your head, you are the weaker interpretation of your name, 'remember me,' said in a plea as though begging not to be erased.

You know you are twenty, and you don't like it. You don't think twenty fits you; you feel more seventeen. You consider seventeen and nineteen to be your forever ages, the ages when you had felt the most *you*. They were also the ages you found yourself in love. You always believed that in your best form, you were love, and in those ages, you were love in the purest way possible. There is something about seventeen and nineteen that is special to you, a certain curve in the ages and the numbers themselves and in you when you were them. Twenty seems like the sharp edge of something, the jagged shards of broken bottles that sank into the external walls of your childhood home. You are giving yourself time though because twenty is still a month old for you. You are giving yourself time to find that familiar curve you had found in your previous ages.

So there you are: twenty-year-old Remember Me in the big red T-shirt, not quite sure of who you are or what you might be. No direction, no love, no thing. What next?

Who are you when no one is looking?

Your door is closed right now, and you are alone in your room. Your parents are talking in the living room. Who are you at this moment?

Your phone doesn't vibrate, and you are at home. For now, you are still Ayemere, or 'Aye', as you have been since you were brought home in a white, frayed blanket from the hospital. The child that brings home grades just short of good and curtsies when she serves her father food on the yellow plastic table that, fifteen years ago, she stood on to reach the sugar container when she knew her mother was far away. She doesn't wake up by 6 a.m. to sweep the compound but still makes sure everywhere is clean, doing just enough to save herself a stern speech from her mother about how people would say she wasn't well-trained, but not enough to become the symbol of obedience other parents would ask their kids to emulate.

In the event that a friend texts or calls, you become AY because the people you keep around you cannot be bothered to say your full name, and you cannot be bothered to insist on it. AY is up for anything. She skips classes to go to the nearest Silverbird Cinema to watch movies she wouldn't focus on, usually because a boy's tongue is down her throat, each boy different from the last. By her feet, another gift they brought to get her attention: a boxed bracelet that upon inspection with the girls she would find out to be fake, a Miss Kay boutique bag with the red dress she put on her Instagram story once, or lingerie because what's more brazen than that? AY likes brazen, and she opens her lips to the audacious. In a group, she is not likely to be seen first, but she is definitely noticed. Her poison is tequila.

You lean further into the bed frame. Are you really seen?

Who really knows you?

You were born at 4:16 p.m. on October 13, 1999, in a dingy hospital in Ikeja with your father and his mother present. You have been multiple people since then. For the first few days, you were 'Baby', because your face was still red and your eyes refused to adjust to the light outside of your mother's cavity. By the time your face lightened to a human-like colour, the naming ceremony had already been held, and your name had become Ayemere. You only allowed your father to carry you, and he did so with pride. With each call of 'Daddy Aye', his lips stretched across his face till they looked like they would tear past his puffy cheeks and keep stretching. You played your part well, making silent gurgles and widening your eyes, so people commented on how much you looked like your father and how beautiful you would be when you grow up. Your father could explode. You remained only Ayemere till an easier name for errands and berating needed to be coined, then you became Aye. You stayed as Aye the longest until you were about to finish secondary school, and the teenage need for reinvention cut you open. AY was born at 11:45 a.m. on May 11, 2015, in the third stall of the boys' bathroom after you finished your last WAEC paper.

You are Ayemere only when you are left alone, such as now, and when you are with Her, or 'were' because you have just been dumped. Not that second, but you are nursing six-month-old wounds that are still as fresh as the day they were cut. You do cut—the scars are all over your yellow thighs—but you are trying not to give in to your whims of self-hate. You are a week into this now.

How long you will go, you don't know yet, but there is a weak determination in you, and you use each day that passes, without you reaching for a blunt pair of scissors, to propel yourself. Your friends don't understand why you won't come out or why you have distanced yourself, but how would they when it did not match the person you had presented to them? They would not understand many things about Ayemere, like how she goes back to watch and understand the movies at Silverbird and how she finds alcohol repulsive. It would not make sense to them that AY and Ayemere are different. They would not understand the scars.

Who really knew you? She does. Did.

You met Her as Ayemere at a place you cannot go to anymore because remembering Her is too painful for you. Even now, you frown and your stomach hurts, but you continue to think because it is necessary for the journey you have started. Ayemere felt alive when She was there, and in a way that accommodated AY and Aye, and She nurtured them. It was with Her that you found out the three parts of you shared traits. You all could draw and you all could sing. You all did not like the foreign texture of sushi. You all loved to be held in your sleep. You even found you could borrow traits from one of the others and go unnoticed. Aye could laugh with AY's friends, and Ayemere was the one that made them laugh, and She was the one that teased it out of you. Your 19th year was spent being a beautiful blend of AY, Aye, and you, with Her and because of Her, because you liked the way She called your real name, Ayemere.

You are unsure of what happened or what caused Her to leave: whether it was because the differences within you became too much for Her to handle, or because She realized She couldn't be with someone who was unsure of herself and always withdrew her hand from Hers when she saw her friends coming. But one day She told you it was over, and you knew it really was. Now you feel as naked as you were on the day of your birth, except this time you are not only in the presence of your parents and grandmother but also of your friends and everyone that has ever met you, and your body is fully formed.

There is no AY or Aye now; there is barely any Ayemere. How can there be when you have seen what it is like to be fully yourself? But what do you do now with the leftovers of the old you that was split into sections for whatever crowd you found yourself in? How could She cut you open and leave you out to bleed? Your mother doesn't understand why this is happening, why you are no longer helping or speaking or sweeping, and you don't understand how she can't see. You can't tell her yourself because it is not something she would ever understand—the three of you and Her—and you are not going to bother trying. Stories of people thrown out of their houses or sent to church for deliverance swim in your head, and you frown. You were never a churchgoer, and it is another thing your mother doesn't know about you.

Your back is beginning to hurt now because you have been angled weirdly. You straighten your posture and look around you. There are pieces of *your* three everywhere. There are AY's heels and Aye's functional sandals. By the bed are the dirty green Crocs that you all agree are comfortable. You make a mental note to clean them later. The cluttered brown desk where you do schoolwork, position your phone to take pictures, and draw is by the window. You haven't drawn since She left. Your papers are now mats for your dying potted succulents.

What would it take you to be yourself?

There are beginnings of an idea germinating in your head. Your spirit and soul are awake, and they refuse to be dormant again. Restlessness brews inside you, and sometimes, you don't know whether you want to cry or scream. So you find yourself in states like this, sitting on your bed and staring into space while your mind races. You can let yourself imagine a different you, one that is whole and complete rather than broken into different pieces for others, but you won't go too far because such a thing does not seem possible for you. What will you do about the change? How will you cope? What will people say? Are you even ready for such a change?

When you were five, you had a Barbie doll. You named her Dorcas after a character in a movie your mum watched repeatedly. She had flowing blonde hair and a shiny pink dress that stopped right above her knee. You spent your playtimes conjuring numerous scenarios for her: Dorcas at the beach with her friends, Gbambose the yellow SpongeBob chair and Henry the teddy bear; Dorcas in her huge mansion watching her favourite show, Teletubbies; Dorcas lounging with her best friend, Lady, who was also a teddy bear.

Whenever you heard roars from the room across yours, you turned to Dorcas and her mansion so huge two people could stand at opposite ends and not see each other. At break time in school, you wouldn't have Dorcas because you weren't allowed to bring dolls, so you thought of her and her band of friends who always had her back, as the other children taunted you. You spent so much time helping Dorcas live her life that you had time for nothing else, and really, what other thing were you going to be doing at five years old? Your mother noticed this, and after a day of drinking Jergens cream smoothies with all her toy friends, Dorcas went missing during your bath time. Your mother told you she went on a long vacation, but even at five, you couldn't be fooled like that. You were turning six the next day. Maybe this is why you prefer odd-numbered ages.

You acknowledge that you have issues with letting go. Why else are you still trying to hold on to succulents that are clearly dead? It is what happened with Dorcas. You didn't let her know, but each time your mother was preoccupied, you searched her room for your doll, hoping that you would see her under sheets of paper or behind a heap of clothes or in a drawer. Even now that you no longer have a need for dolls and you have since moved from that house, you think about finding her with the shiny pink dress you last saw her in. It is what is happening now with AY and Aye. In a world bereft of safety and stability, you found solace in your malleable personality, and now it seems you are being forced to gain rigidity, choose a person to be.

You're not even sure you like your options.

To be Aye, you would have to be the devoted daughter, the 'chosen one' as your father would say. You would have to be somebody worth remembering and that means following every rule of life society has given you: BSc and MSc holder (preferably with honours) with a well-paying job, enough for you to fend for yourself but not so much that a man gets intimidated; married to a good man of your parents' approval by twenty-five, latest twenty-seven, children by thirty-two so your mother can fulfil her *omugwo* dreams; devoted mother and wife who caters to her new and old families' needs till the day she too can place those responsibilities on her daughter and become a player in the never-ending cycle. Aye would have safety, security in her societal stance, and her legacy would be her undying faithfulness right from the moment she was born and decided to stay.

The alternative, AY, is not much different. Despite AY's exuberance, she is a well-grounded individual who balances work and play. As AY, you would party hard and work hard. You would have your own money and live by your terms to some extent. You might not get married by twenty-five but you would, maybe by twenty-nine or your early thirties. You would probably marry one of your recurrent conquests with a flashy job and a big house your parents would proudly say belongs to their in-law. Maybe later in life you would hang up your heels and let yourself slip into some features of Aye because you would need rest. Your ankles might ache, but you would not suffer. You would be okay.

Ayemere would be met with wrath once you decide you want to be her, your true self. First of all, you would abandon the finance degree you're in school for and begin again in fine arts; then you would dye your hair some outrageous colour and pierce your nose. You would tell your parents the things that eat up your chest, and you would swallow their bitter replies. You might have to move out; actually, they would kick you out, and you would have to fend for yourself. 'Disappointment' would be slapped across your face, figuratively and literally.

You are breathing heavily now. These thoughts do not sit well with you. You think of how, with Ayemere, there would be other Shes or maybe She herself. Your breathing eases up a bit, but you clench your stomach. You are thinking about Her again.

What parts of you will be remembered? How do you want to be remembered?

You hear your mother's voice. She is calling for Aye to put the soup she cooked earlier into containers. You slip on your Crocs and head to the kitchen. You must take care of the soup now, or it will spoil. Egusi does not tolerate nonsense.

ROSES OF SKIN AND IRON
Deborah Vuha

'Unbelievable!' Ivy Ocansey storms out the hall. The plates on her tray clatter in rhythm with her clicking heels as she ducks into the kitchen. 'After all that work!'

Her husband stops at the foot of the stairs, hands on his hips. He raises an eyebrow at the kitchen doorway. 'What's the drama queen's problem now?'

'Oh.' Sitting cross-legged on the couch, their daughter swallows the last of her turkey sandwich. 'She made me yam and *kontomire*, but my belly has no more room.'

'Ivy,' the word is a whine he carries into the kitchen, 'you know Rosa doesn't like to feel too full before a match.'

'But it's at ten, Mawuli. 10 a.m.' In a cloud of lemon perfume, Ivy flounces back into the hall and stops beside her daughter. Rosa's innocent eyes stay on the TV where a US Open classic is showing. 'And just because it says she plays at 10 doesn't mean she starts at 10. There could be rain—'

'It's an indoor court,' Rosa says.

'The match before yours could last beyond three hours—'

'It's four games to win a set and three sets to win a match.'

'And deuce is both game point and break point, so the games will be shorter,' Mawuli says from the kitchen, around a mouthful.

Ivy crosses her arms beneath her bosom. 'You two plan to shoot down all my—'

'Ma.' Rosa sets her plate on the centre table and stands. She cups Ivy's upper arms. 'Relax. I'll be alright.'

The sight of Rosa's smile is too taxing on Ivy's anger. 'Fine,' she says on the back of a sigh. 'But if you faint, you'll hear it.' Her gaze rises to Rosa's forehead and lingers on the gnarled triangle that isn't quite skin. The younger woman can guess what her Mother's words will be. 'Wear a sweatband.'

Rosa bites her itchy bottom lip, wishing it were as easy to quell the itch that's begun in her gut. 'You know it interferes with my space buns.'

'Rosa.' She winces as her mother's fingers dig into her forearms. 'When you're on the court I don't want people to see that—' her eyes flick upward '—and judge you. I want them to respect you, not decide you're—'

'Ma.' Rosa's eyes drift closed. For a few agonizing seconds, she's treated to the deafening sound of her frantic heartbeat. Those parts of her body that are still flesh prickle. The familiar unwelcome tentacles of doubt spiral up her legs and threaten to squeeze out every last shred of self-belief.

Breathe.

She opens her eyes. 'Relax.' Her lips contort into a smile, like they've become accustomed to doing the past six years when she chooses to ignore the reality of what the E-Waste Explosion of '21 did to her. 'I've gotten this far, Ma. When I get on the court, my racket will speak.'

Ivy's eyes search her daughter's as if looking for traces of uncertainty. Rosa's spine stiffens in anticipation of further argument. But her mother's arms wind around her. With the sudden onslaught of relief, it's all Rosa can do to keep from collapsing against Ivy's chest. 'Make me proud,' Ivy whispers, before kissing the top of her daughter's head.

'When haven't I?'

'Oh, spare me.' Over her shoulder, Ivy calls, 'Mawuli? Come and take your daughter to the Club!'

The Abena Maitland Racket Club locker room thrums to the beat of slamming medicine balls and whirring gym equipment. Athletes, some spurred on by their coaches, engage in sprints, box jumps and lunges, prepping themselves for the final day of Qualifiers for the 2027 Maitland-Accra Open. The air crackles with grunts, perfume, and the faint waft of perspiration.

From where she straddles a stationary bike, pedalling at a punishing speed, Rosa tries without success to keep her eyes off the twenty-one-year-old doing resistance band drills a few feet away. France's Bernadette Pascal, who defeated the Australian Open 2024 champion, Margery Rutherford, in straight sets, is the number three seed and Rosa's next opponent.

Rosa lowers her head, her focus on the hands that clutch the handlebars. She'll be kidding if she says she isn't a little intimidated, awestruck even. She's dreamed of winning the Australian Open for longer than she's understood how Grand Slams work, and this is her first WTA tournament. Pascal defeated a defending champion! Her form may have dipped since, but if the bagels she's dished out in her previous qualifiers say anything, it's that you best not let your guard down around her.

Fresh adrenaline surges through Rosa at the thought of sharing a court with Pascal. She's already played two qualifiers herself, dropping only one set. Pascal is her greatest challenge yet, but the warrior within Rosa, who's lived half her life on a court, believes she can beat her.

'Hey, Scrap Metal Girl's here early. That's cute.'

For a second, one so long she's sure it's been noticed, Rosa's legs freeze. Anger clouds her excitement, and she has to shut her eyes and focus on slowing down her breathing. She doesn't need to look to know that the words are for her, or who the honeyed voice belongs to, here to taunt her for the third day in a row.

'Sala, be nice.' Ah, her second in command is there too. 'Maybe when the robot uprising starts, she'll pity us.'

A few choice words threaten to tumble out Rosa's mouth. She bites them down. It's not the first time she's been called a robot. It won't be the last. She has the E-Waste Explosion of '21 to thank.

In 2020 the Ghanaian government admitted that the electronic waste dumpsite at Agbogbloshie was a health hazard. They decided to replace it with a reprocessing plant, and in under a year, following the hardest—and quickest—the citizens had ever seen contractors work, the plant stood, glorious and proud, in the space that used to be a junkyard. The proprietors were so proud; they opened the facility up to anyone who wanted to visit. It was welcome news to schools that had slots in their calendars for excursions and not enough money to make those excursions good.

On August 11, 2021, Rosa, twenty-nine of her classmates, and two teachers from Saint Elizabeth Junior High visited this place of wonder where old computer parts were remade into game consoles and phones. On August 11, 2021, an overworked factory hand spilt petrol over exposed wiring, starting a gruesome domino effect. On August 11, 2021, the Agbogbloshie Reprocessing Plant exploded, lighting up the sky in a macabre firework display.

Between the victims' ruptured skins and punctured internal organs, the doctors knew this was a disaster of unseen proportions. But while they tore at their hair, weird things happened in the ICU. Skin regrew. Lungs, livers, kidneys with bits blown off in the blast, became whole again. But the new bits weren't made from human tissue. They were malleable strips of varied metals, like those recycled in the reprocessing plant. Of the ninety-one people involved in the blast, seventy-two survived but at the cost of living with large areas of skin an inhuman colour, which withstood all attempts at makeup, and some half-metal internal organs of questionable functionality.

Some people accepted the survivors. Some said they accepted them but put their hands over their kids' eyes if any of them came near. Some displayed open disgust. Six years on, Rosa's learned to grin and bear it. It doesn't get easier with repetition.

She gets off the bike, whips her phone out of her pocket, and saunters off in her best impression of nonchalance. 'Oh, a word of advice, dear.' Rosa presses her lips together and keeps moving, so Salamat shouts the rest of it. 'Don't take a shower after your match! We wouldn't want you getting electrocuted!'

The phone vibrates in her hand, a welcome distraction to the sound of laughter behind her. A look at the caller ID makes her skin prickle, in a different way from when her mother accidentally reminded her she was a scrap metal kid. 'Hey,' she says when she answers.

His smile on the screen is so bright he could be in the room. 'I should be there,' Alexander Hagan says.

'Fans aren't allowed for qualifiers.'

'Fans?' His brow quirks. 'I'm your coach!'

She chuckles. Hitting partner is more accurate. Three years her senior, Alexander's been her friend since she was four, when she wandered into his yard looking for her doll's stiletto. That he still remembers her now, when he's hogging the spotlight for defending his title in Madrid, thrills her. 'You have an exam. At ten.'

The twenty-two-year-old shrugs. 'So? I have money. What will education do for me?' When Alex smiles again, she pats one of her low space buns, for want of something to do with her suddenly fidgety hands. 'You ready?'

Rosa glances over her shoulder. Pascal shuffles on the balls of her feet between two cones, her yellow shirt crinkling with each swing she practises. She's a beast, and the court is her jungle.

Rosa has never wanted to be on the court so badly.

'I'm ready.'

'First set, Bernadette Pascal to serve.'

Beneath the white lights on the arched roof of Centre Court, Rosa waits behind the baseline. She bends forward, twirling the handle of her racket as she rocks from side to side on the balls of her feet. She's not wearing the sweatband; her white long-sleeved blouse and matching capris hide the bulk of the blotches on her skin. Her eyes stay on the woman bouncing a tennis ball on the other side of the court. She springs up as soon as Pascal tosses the ball above her head.

The first serve is a rocket that ricochets off the service line and out of court quicker than Rosa's racket can touch it. 'Fifteen-love,' the chair umpire announces. Rosa blinks. She walks to the left of the baseline, slapping her thigh for encouragement. When Pascal fires the next one, Rosa gets her racket on the ball. It flies into the tramlines. She manages to get a return on Bernadette's next serve, but a drop shot catches her off-guard. 'Forty-love.'

'You knew it would be difficult,' Rosa mutters. 'Now work!'

Pascal's next serve is powerful. Rosa's return is a sitting duck. Pascal's shoes pound the concrete as she sprints to the net to hit a volley. It's long. 40-15. Rosa lets out a low whistle as she walks to the other side of the centre mark, wondering how she's still in the game. The holiday's short-lived when Pascal makes use of classic misdirection and fires a winner behind Rosa in the next point. 'Game, Pascal.'

'It's only the first game.' It's the chant Rosa repeats to herself as she jogs to her bench for water before they switch sides. When she serves, endorphins that were absent two minutes before rush through her bloodstream. Her feet are fluid as she and her opponent engage in the match's first extended rally. The fifteen shot point ends when Pascal hits a backhand into the net. Rosa would prefer to start her service games with aces, but she'll take winning the point.

Two ill-timed errors rattle Rosa. When she double-faults at 15-30, she slams her racket butt-first on the concrete. It bobs back up, and she snatches it by the strings, rolling her eyes as the umpire issues a warning.

She spares a glance at her opponent, then launches a missile that strikes the centre service line before bouncing out of Pascal's reach. 'Thirty-forty.' She jogs in place before serving again, and shuffles out of the way as Pascal's return misses the baseline by inches. 'Deuce.'

Another rally begins. When Pascal sticks her racket out to send forward another drop shot, Rosa flies up the court, only slowing when the ball hits the net and falls on Pascal's side. 'One game all.'

The analyst in Rosa takes over. Pascal's sweet spot is the baseline; she prefers dictating play from there, hitting long, aggressive balls deep into the court. Her serve is strong, but she doesn't know how to rein in her power. Short balls would force her to the net and exploit her tendency to over-hit.

A half-volley earns Rosa a break point, and she forces a forehand miss from Bernadette.

'Game, Ocansey. Ocansey leads two games to one.'

Match point.

It's the first match point on Rosa's serve, her fourth in total; she got complacent at 15-40 in Pascal's last service game. She leads the third set tiebreak 6-5, and if she knows anything about tennis, it's that she can still lose.

She serves. The ball is a yellow blur that flies into no man's land. 'Fault!'

Her fingers tighten on the racket to crush the urge to smash it. In the one hour and twenty-two minutes they've played, she's learned two things: her second serve is weak, and Bernadette Pascal knows how to pounce on them. Rosa will have to hit a wild second serve. It's a stupid risk.

What better time to take a stupid risk than when her career depends on it?

She fires the ball down the T for her ninth ace.

'Game, set, match, Rosa Ocansey.'

'Great game, Ocansey.'

Rosa closes her locker and swivels to face Bernadette, the only other person in the locker room now that five of today's six matches have been played and most of the women have left. 'I was playing the prodigy that beat Marge Rutherford,' Rosa says, grinning. 'I had to bring my A-game.'

'Please.' Bernadette laughs airily. 'Your forehands were blistering! You hit an ace of two hundred and eight kilometres per hour.'

'You're joking!'

'Oh, but I'm not. Truly impressive. Then again, it's the kind of thing we should expect, you know, from your . . . kind.'

Rosa's chest tightens. 'Excuse me?'

Bernadette's shoulders heave. 'I heard about your accident. Who knows? Maybe it gave you some—' she lifts her hands to draw air quotes '—enhanced abilities.'

Rosa can't hold back a surprised laugh. 'What?'

Bernadette slips one hand into the pocket of her pink skirt. 'Think about it. The media definitely will.'

Rosa licks her lips. They don't moisten. 'What are you—'

'Oh, *chérie*.' Bernadette claws through her shoulder-length hair. 'The media will ask all sorts of questions. When I beat Marge, it was exciting! One day I was an invisible girl from Nantes. The next day people wanted to know my favourite breakfast cereal! And who doesn't like attention?' She sighs. 'But when they started interfering, asking whether that date I went on the other night was the reason why I lost a match or if I could be into drugs because a friend of mine was arrested for drink-driving, that's when I knew those people were cruel.' She lays a hand on her chest. 'And I'm normal. What would they do to you?'

The veins in Rosa's neck throb. 'How dare you?'

'No, no.' Bernadette puts her hand on Rosa's shoulder and doesn't notice when the other woman flinches. 'I'm saving you. The WTA is huge. The media will strip you naked for their entertainment. You threw your racket. They'll say your accident gave you violent tendencies.'

And that's different from what she hears every day? 'So? Let them.'

Bernadette taps her chin. 'Withdraw from the tournament.'

A corner of Rosa's lips curls in a wry smile. 'So you can get in as a lucky loser?'

Bernadette smiles. 'To save yourself. They haven't robbed you of your peace yet. Don't give them the chance.'

The chill in the bus is a pleasant contrast to the heat of mid-afternoon Accra. Rosa sits at the back, reruns of her conversation with Bernadette interfering with the country music coming in through her earbuds. Her phone beeps as her father's text comes in: *Think I left my pen drive on your mother's dresser. Send me the file in the Beta folder when you get home.*

Behind the driver's seat, a rectangular sheet of glass slices through the air as it slides down from a slot in the ceiling, stopping when all 16-by-20 inches of it is visible. It flicks on to reveal a familiar montage of a spinning globe, the chirpy jingle of the one o'clock news filling the transit bus. Rosa plucks out an earbud, although her gaze stays on the houses floating by in the light traffic outside.

'Police interrupted a bank robbery this morning . . .'

She pushes the earbud back in and lets her eyes flutter shut.

'. . . is a survivor of the E-Waste Explosion of 2021.'

Rosa's eyes snap open. Her head jerks in the direction of the screen where there's a still shot of a man and the caption: 'Man Arrested For Attempted Bank Robbery.' She doesn't know him, but the jagged, uneven patches of grey and red in his brown skin tell her enough. He was in the blast.

'Those people!' The picture makes way for a video of a trembling woman hugging herself, a microphone thrust below her nose. 'If they're even still people. Show me one of them that acts normal. It's like the blast messed with their minds! That monster took us hostage. He should be locked in an asylum. All of his kind!'

'Sure,' Rosa whispers, her eyes returning to the window. 'Because before the blast nobody committed crimes.'

The bus's doors whoosh open to let in more passengers. Out of habit, Rosa looks around.

And instantly wishes she didn't.

Everyone is staring at her. The red triangle embedded in the tan skin of her temple, the grey flecks on her jawline, and the burn scars on her neck have not gone unnoticed. The driver keeps his eyes on the windshield, but his conductor makes up for it by, like everyone else, regarding Rosa with suspicious eyes. Their bodies are tense, as if ready to bolt should the unpredictable robot child have an episode.

Her skin burns under their scrutiny. She squirms. The man in the seat across the aisle tightens his fingers around his briefcase.

The chill in the bus is a painful contrast to the heat of her body. She stands, ignoring that her house is a half-hour away, and lugs her tennis bag onto her shoulders by the straps. The words from the TV ebb into oblivion. Her laboured breathing is all she hears. People burrow into the side of the bus as she walks past.

'Monster!'

Rosa doesn't look back to see who said it. Like a stray she can't shake, the word bobs around in her head all through her walk home.

'Incoming video call,' the disembodied voice of the Ocansey household's virtual assistant announces.

Rosa returns the bottle of eye drops to her bedside drawer, blinking down the last of the sting in her eyes. Who still calls landlines? 'Who is it?'

'Alexander Hagan.'

'Answer.'

There's a hum as one of her bedroom walls morphs into the view from the Hagans' kitchen. Alexander sits on the island, scooping diced fruit from a clear bowl into his mouth, a white T-shirt hugging his muscled torso. His brown skin glistens with sweat. 'Your bedroom hasn't changed,' he says, his lips in an amused crescent.

'Liar.' It's one of the rare times that seeing him does nothing to her insides. 'I changed the drapes from sky blue to navy.'

He shakes his head. 'Anyway. My coach is in town tomorrow—' He stops, his eyes narrowing. 'Are you okay?'

Rosa's teeth rake her upper lip. 'Bernadette said I have enhanced abilities.'

Alex chuckles. 'I should hope so. You train with a world-class athlete.'

Her left shoulder rises. 'I think I should quit.'

The video zooms in on him till he's visible only from the chest up. The light dusting of freckles across his nose is so close she can count them. 'What?'

'Can I tell you a secret?'

'Of course.'

'I haven't looked in a mirror in five years.' She leaps off the bed and begins to pace, her heart thudding to the beat of her rising anguish. 'Five months. That's how long I was in the hospital after the blast. When I came back it took another month before I could haul myself out of bed. And I looked in the mirror.' She stops. Her palms drag down her face. 'And I knew I didn't want to see that again.' She looks at him. 'Not my face. Not my body.'

His eyes don't leave hers as he sets down the bowl. 'Rosa—'

'And everyday people remind me why.' She continues pacing. 'They look at me, and they cringe. Or run. If this were a movie I could just save someone, and they'll all love me. Instead, someone like me just tried to rob a bank! As far as everyone's concerned I'm just like him! The blast must have done something. That's what they say. Messed with my head. Made me violent. At any point I could just erupt and go on a murderous spree!'

'Not everyone—'

'And I look the part! I'm a monster!'

Alex sighs. 'You're not a monster.'

She yanks her sweater over her head, flings it on the bed and turns crazed eyes to an open-mouthed Alex. She stands in her sports bra and trousers, her outstretched arms forming a crucifix. 'Look at me!' She's one of the few survivors whose faces weren't excessively damaged. But, covering the length of her arms, stretching downward from her collarbone, patches of black and grey metal appear in a haphazard sequence. They're wedged deep within the skin, leaving her flesh in uneven bumps and depressions, as though a sculptor ran out of clay while making her. 'Tell me you don't see a monster.'

A bit of her heart crumbles for every second Alexander remains mute.

'You can't.' Her pacing resumes. 'Like, what am I even? A person? A mutant? A serial killer in waiting because of this mess the blast is supposed to have made my brain? Did you know that beyond potentially being a criminal, I only have full capacity of one lung? That they installed two shelves in my bathroom to carry the medicines I need to live? That my life falling apart is a good reason to cry, but I can't because the explosion fried my tear ducts?'

'Rosa—'

'The scientists said they'd figure out a safe cosmetic procedure for us. Have they? No!' She throws her hands up. 'It's been six years, Alex! Six! What have they done since? They're more interested in sticking us under their lenses and marvelling at the freakish cockroaches we've become!'

He jumps off the kitchen island. 'I'm coming over.'

'Why?' She stops, her throat inflamed with the effort it takes to breathe.

His brows wrinkle. 'You're going through a rough time. That's not reason enough?'

'Why do you stick around?' She wants to stop speaking. She can't. 'I get that my family does. They're burdened with me. Most of the town seems to have ostracized me. What about you? Is it pity? Does being friends with the dregs of society make you feel more saintly?'

His lips part. When she sees the hurt in his eyes, the floor sways beneath her. 'You think I'm your friend because I pity you?' It's a whisper. It's louder than anything she's heard all day.

There's a hum as the call disconnects.

The icon labelled 'Rosa' catches her eye when she turns on her father's computer. Her forefinger hovers over it for all of two seconds, and then she taps.

Videos. Her eyes balloon as she scans the folder. It's dotted with hundreds of videos. Her skin breaks out in gooseflesh when she recognizes herself in the thumbnails. They cover various stages of her growth, some of them showing her as a laughing baby, the more recent ones showing her as a young adult with blotchy skin. Her swallow is audible as she taps on the most recent video.

It opens up to the lush interior of Mawuli's Volvo. He flashes the peace sign when he's in view, then switches to the other camera.

Rosa sits in the passenger seat, her eyes on the fists in her lap. 'What do we tell ourselves before the match?' he asks.

Rosa licks her lips. 'I have many talents, and today I'll use them.'

'And?'

'I'm a strong woman. I rise above every challenge.'

'And?'

'I deserve success. I deserve happiness.'

I'm a strong woman. I deserve success.

On the side of the Club's one outdoor court, Rosa sits cross-legged on a bench, the stars winking down at her as the two sentences turn over in her head. The pre-match ritual of positive affirmations is Mawuli's idea, and she's only gone along with it to make him happy, never really giving the words much thought. Now, when she thinks of quitting, those words force her to take notice.

The bench squeaks as it bears another weight. 'The audacity.'

His gravelly voice already gave him away, but she turns to look anyway. Alex sits on her left, dressed in a black T-shirt, white shorts and sneakers, his striped tennis bag at his feet. He taps his right foot to a rhythm only he hears. She scratches the back of her ear. 'If this is about me saying you're friends with me out of pity—'

'Apologize.'

'Why? It could've been hunger talking.'

'Then again, why start apologizing now? You didn't when you stole my racket.'

'You broke my doll!'

'I was weaning you off dolls.'

'I was five!'

'Exactly! Old enough.'

'You're a sick man.'

They watch the court in silence, their thoughts occasionally interrupted by distant caws or the rev of an engine.

'For the record, I don't think you're a freak.' He fingers his neckline. 'You just . . . like country music. Nobody's perfect.'

'Bernadette said not to let them steal my peace.' Rosa rubs her palms together, but the ice in her bones stays. 'Considering everything that happens in my life, that seems like sound advice.'

'What is your peace, Rosa? Look.' The floral notes of his cologne are more pronounced as Alex shifts closer. 'I won't lie. Professional tennis can be insanely brutal. You will doubt yourself! Expect it! You know what will keep you above your competition?' His hand covers hers, their fingers interlacing. 'Mental toughness.'

His eyes hold an earnestness that makes her glad to be sitting. 'When you couldn't move, for all those months, I didn't know if you'd ever play again. Or if you'd ever walk again.' His voice is unnervingly raw. 'But you did. Your body took a while to adjust. But you showed up to the court with your racket every day. You didn't care when people bullied you. You're the most iron-willed person I know. Nothing beats you down.' His hand squeezes hers. 'I get it. You're questioning who you are because of Bernadette and other recent events.' His head inches closer. 'But have you ever doubted that this is what you want to do? Can you imagine doing anything else?'

She peels her gaze from his, long enough to stare at the blue court bathed in a shower of LED lights. It's her favourite place. The thought of returning to the court was one of the ropes she clutched to get through the frustration of being bedridden for six months. She's scraped time between classes to play tennis, with her father, with Alex, with trainers who weren't too repulsed to coach her. Her racket has become an extension of her arm.

This is her peace.

'I can't stop.' Joy bursts within her like a popped balloon. 'I don't want to.' In a world that hasn't stopped reminding her that she teeters between human and spare parts, her identity on the court is the one thing she has never doubted. 'This is who I am.'

'Good.' His smile is triumphant. 'Plus, if you quit, you'll never get to beat me in mixed doubles.'

'I do want to beat you in doubles!'

'Hm.' Alex bends to unzip his bag. 'Yet you needed four match points to close out today's match. Disgraceful!' He places a racket on her lap and rises. 'Stand up.'

She fixes him a pointed stare. 'This isn't so much about my match point conversion rate as it is about you preparing for the Rogers Cup, is it?'

Alex winks. 'I can multitask.'

I rise above every challenge.

Bag strapped to her back, Rosa waves as she steps out of the tunnel onto Centre Court to the sound of cheers, blinking back her surprise at how full the stadium is. She laughs when she sees her player box. Her parents, who have both chosen to work from home today so they can in fact watch her live, are practically jumping. Alex stops taking pictures with fans long enough to beam at her.

I'm a strong woman. She puts her bag on her bench and joins her opponent on the court for the coin toss. Standing there, racket in hand, the sound of an excited crowd around her, the prospect of a match: it feels like home.

I'm a tennis player. It's what she was born to do. It's what she wants to do. And no one is going to take it away from her.

Not if her iron will have anything to do with it.

HEAVY RAINS
Prosper Wilton Makara

The story that I have been asked to tell does not start with Tapiwa's irrevocable psychosis nor his subsequent imprisonment. It would also be depressing for this story to start with the finality of death. Although this narrative will inevitably lead us there, it is not necessarily all about that. Things began to fall apart when my brother, Tapiwa, assaulted Brito—Brito, the madman who roamed the streets of the insular Domboshava stark naked, his disproportionately large penis swooshing left-right, left-right. Tales of Brito's large manhood abound—some more realistic than others—the most famous being that he got the ugly, jagged scar that ran on the left side of his face from Ba' Ruva after the latter caught the former atop his wife, having the ride of his life. The truth is Mai Ruva had been told by Sekuru Muchawa to get a madman's semen.

A common tale in townships: madmen's semen used as an ingredient in love potions to lull one's husband, to make him docile and not leave. This tale of the portentous nature of *Weti yeGudo* and *Chipotanemadziro* is a long story that requires a thick volume of its own.

It was also common knowledge that Brito was clairvoyant, with a natural inclination for fatalistic news. He had led people to

Russo and his gang, who were running an intricate cattle rustling syndicate. Brito had also told the Malawian kid from across our house, Chibwana, that the earth would swallow him 'on the day in which noon was night'. And as sure as the day was day, Chibwana died during a solar eclipse.

Now, the link between the two—Brito's assault and the ensuing fracas—is still questionable, but I have to confess that, since then, I have had to revise my beliefs. I have become a little less questioning of the power of deities that pull at the strings of fate.

Perhaps I should be a little less theatrical and tell you the story as it happened.

My mother had four children, three sons and a daughter. Having this many sons meant that she had firmly planted herself as my father's wife. In our culture, all children are blessings from above but sons are more so than daughters. Sons carry on the family name, unlike daughters who, although they bring wealth in the form of cows when they get married, never truly belong to the family. Their presence is considered transient; they are sojourners, temporarily sheltered as they are groomed for their husbands. My mother, having truly established herself, became like other senior wives: a little complacent, arrogant even.

Having these sons did not mean she was safe from small houses, what the Americans refer to as mistresses, more elevated than a simple fling but less than a wife. Small houses were common. So common that they were a part of every household in both the townships and the suburbs. As it was, by the time I was in grade four, I already knew that my father had several women on the side and many other children. We never talked about them, but their presence hovered over us like deities. My father was not discrete, did not even attempt to be; he left clues, clues that would have riled any sane wife. But my mother was a traditional woman. She accepted that it was only normal for a man to have other women on the side, that it was in men's nature to be polygamous. So, even though Father dangled these affairs in our faces, Mother kept her silence. When she found the occasional condom in the pockets of his safari suits, she muttered that he was at least using protection. 'Not like those fools who just stick it in without protection,' she'd say to Pamela, her young sister. My poor mother, ever so pliant and gentle, was not like her sister, Mainini Pamela, whose effervescence, though contagious, bordered on obnoxiousness. Mainini Pamela who once, in a family court and with a straight face, patted her crotch and shouted, '*Apa, pakasungwa neutare.* No one ever truly leaves after being between my legs.'

We grew up in the township of Glen View. Do not let the anglicized name fool you; the township is a high-density suburb popularly known, for one reason or another, as Location or, as dubbed by the Shona people, *Rokesheni*. Our house was indistinguishable from the others in the street. Small four-roomed houses with a small squat toilet at the back. The majority of the houses had small picket fences, and very few had durawalls. Many houses were cramped into a small space, which meant that we grew up being intimate with our neighbours in ways we would otherwise have chosen not to be. We knew what they ate, or more specifically, what they did not eat. For instance, Gogo Moyo and her family seemed to survive solely on the leafy vegetables that she grew in her backyard and Lameck's wife always burnt whatever she cooked. Living in such proximity, we also knew when Ba' Ruva fought with his wife or when Ma' Shero quarrelled with her husband; she'd shout at the top of her lungs, 'Stupid man, you should work as a normal man would. *Kushaya nyadzi*, you want to be fed by your wife?' Poor man he was, Ba' Shero, with his slight nature and terrible stutter.

In the afternoons, the air was filled with a cacophony of sounds only specific to townships: the shouts of mothers calling their children, children playing *maflawu* and *raka-raka* on the road, children wailing on their mothers' backs, women in nondescript dresses and headwraps gossiping over fences, and the occasional fights when things got a bit feisty.

My family rented three rooms: a bedroom, a sitting room (that doubled as a kitchen and bedroom for the boys), and the girls' bedroom that we called *speya*. It only occurred to me quite recently how absurd this was. Calling it a spare room suggested that we had many rooms and had one left to spare, which was not the case. I remember how we, the boys, would remove the small coffee table from the centre of the sitting room before we laid blankets on the hard floor. An uncomfortable maroon-coloured mat, made from a particularly rough and itchy material, carpeted the floor. We did not have much either: our most valuable possessions were a small, off-white fridge that gave off a constant hum. A hum which became the soundtrack to our meals and those terrible, terrible fights between Mother and Father, those fights in which Father pummelled Mother with his monstrous fists and household appliances flew from one end of the house to the other.

The speya did not have a bed; the only furniture in the room was a wardrobe. The wardrobe had once belonged to my parents at the turn of the decade, and the doors hung uneasily on their hinges and did not close all the way. The shelves had also given way such that they were suspended at precarious angles. Given our numbers, some of us, the youngest ones mostly, had our clothes thrown in a corner and the eldest two used the wardrobe. The speya was also perfumed by the pungent smell of urine as our young, orphaned cousin, Miriam, whom we lived with those days, still wet the blankets. In the morning they would be thrown on fences to dry.

Back then, it never occurred to me that we were poor. We were poor without knowing it, perhaps because everyone around us was the same. Boys with their shorts torn and tattered, usually with holes around the buttocks, hollered about the streets with their chapped buttocks peeking out. The kids also had trousers that had holes between their legs that it was not unusual to find their little penises poking out. The trousers were usually frayed around the knees too, from playing with bricks that they pushed as makeshift toy cars. We grew up in this life, in the same low-income bracket as our neighbours. We could have had reasonably easier lives had we been the only family to be fended for, but my father's status as the eldest son automatically meant that he was also the provider for his other family. He provided for his unemployed siblings and their family, and as years passed, his meagre earnings were stretched to include his mistresses and beer, habits that led to his untimely and devastating demise.

My earliest memories of our family consist of our joy rides in Father's shiny yellow Citroën, family days at Greenwood Park, thick layers of jam on bread, and pure unmasked bliss. I remember we used to laugh more, Father was still our father, and Mother was still her best self. I remember we had easy conversations in the sitting room, our voices unrestrained, and when Father's Citroën hooted at the gate after his workday, we jostled to be the first to hug him, shouting, '*mauya.*'

When I was young, I thought of Tapiwa as an exacting person, rigid in his self-righteousness. He always enjoyed his ability to exercise his little tyrannies over us. He was a law unto himself. He was the kind of person who always wanted things done his way and being the first-born son gave him authority. This status meant that he was highly favoured and got away with just about anything. The almighty Tapiwa who never erred. Everyone pampered him, and to our chagrin, all his little mischiefs were quickly forgiven.

Tapiwa also often took it upon himself to chastise us: 'It is my duty as your elder brother,' he'd often say as the cane descended repeatedly and unforgivingly on our unclothed bottoms, leaving welts that made it hard for us to sit for a day or two. This might sound like the most shocking abuse to you, but it is not in the least bit unusual, particularly in the townships. We all turned out fine. Except, of course, Tapiwa who is now incarcerated at Chikurubi Maximum Prison as I speak. He is going to appeal though because the lawyer I found him is arguing that there are extenuating circumstances to his case that warrant a lesser sentence.

In the year 2001, when I was in second grade, Tonderai fourth grade, Tariro fifth, and Tapiwa had just finished his Grade Seven examinations, we went to visit *Gogo* in Domboshava for the Christmas holidays. I always looked forward to time spent with Gogo in Domboshava, the insular village with its slow life and cool, thatched huts.

We travelled in our Sunday best, the boys in Jean dungarees and Tariro in a pink dress with red poppies all over. For shoes, we all wore Sandak and felt proud at the envious glares of our friends as we boarded the bus. Our mother had asked Ba' Ruva to accompany us to Fourth Street from where we would get the second bus to Domboshava.

You are probably wondering why I have chosen to tell you about Domboshava. Well, Domboshava was the tipping point. The place where things ceased to be as they should have been. Had I the power, I would go back to 2001, that particular holiday in Molife, Domboshava, and stop the terrible things that happened.

Gogo was ageless. Her eyes were pools of wisdom and warmth, and her gait sturdy. She moved around with an urgency uncharacteristic of one so old.

Now that I am older, I have tried, at times, to imagine my mother growing up in Domboshava as a chubby toddler, her fat chin wet with dripping saliva. I have tried to imagine what her toothless grin would have been like, but I cannot conjure such an image. I have tried to imagine what it would have been like for her to wake up at dawn, fetch water from the river, sweep the compound, and cook on the open hearth. I cannot.

You see, by the time I was old enough to know my right from my left, I realized that my mother was unhappy. Mother became, to me, like a china doll, very fragile and dainty. It was as if she could simply bump into a wall, break into two, and die. Mother wore her sorrow around her sleeves and desperation as cologne. There were times when she would stare blankly into space. You could talk and talk, and she would not hear you. You could scream, and she would not hear you still. During the weekends that Father was home, her eyes glazed over, and she moved from room to room like a ghost, lifeless. This is why it is hard for me to picture Gogo giving birth to her. Gogo with her fluidity and briskness could have been my father's mother. Our father was a man of hurried interactions. It was as if he was always late for something: the way he left early in the morning in his long, confident strides to his Citroën, the brusqueness in his conversations that at times left you wondering what he had just said. Father was not a man you could question or ask to repeat himself.

Anyway, during this particular holiday, Tapiwa became insufferable, much more than he already was. We had to wake up early, very early, around five in the morning so that we could till Gogo's maize field in that awfully large strip of land behind her corrugated zinc-roofed bedroom. This was the only part we hated about holidays in Domboshava, this ritualistic early morning hoeing. To make matters worse, this particular holiday, Gogo let Tapiwa stay behind at home under the pretext of studying, which was odd. What could our cunning Tapiwa be studying when he had just finished his Grade Seven exams that year? However, Gogo, being uneducated herself, treated education with awe and a resigned acceptance that it could never be hers. So, Tapiwa, just like our sister Tariro who only had to follow after sweeping the compound, was always left at home while we hoed in the field, interacting with itchy weeds and caterpillars.

We kept quiet, channelling our fury into our work so that only the repeated thump-thump of the hoe hitting the moist soil groaned in the morning air, our resentment burning holes in our throats. Our only comfort was that even though we had to endure this gruesome task until the sun was well above our heads, we would soon leave the field to go play soccer.

If we were lucky, best-case-scenario lucky, we could sneak out unnoticed by Tapiwa—who, I swear, was fussier than our parents—and go swim in Mukwadzi River. But that flicker of hope was usually dampened by Tapiwa whom we often found sitting under the cool shade of a mango tree, sucking the sweet and delicious juice of the fruit, some of it the trickling down his hand and the front of his red Billabong T-Shirt. He would give us that evil snigger of his and, if Gogo was well out of earshot, say something like, 'How was your day, peasants?' I did not know what the word peasant meant, but the way he said it made me choke on an ugly emotion I could not name. I could not do anything because of my age; I knew if I lost my temper and tried to attack, Tapiwa would cane me until I had welts as big as those mangoes. Unlike me, Tonde was adamant. He often fell for the bait and would retort sharply in response. Even though he managed to throw a few punches at Tapiwa here and there, he was always beaten. I never really knew if this ritual of challenging Tapiwa daily was bravery or stupidity, but I will not lie, I always enjoyed those few punches that landed on Tapiwa.

Something unexpected happened after one particularly arduous day of labouring in the field. We got home to find Tapiwa at his usual spot under the mango tree. On this day, however, he was not eating a mango but making a toy car from wires, his brows furrowed in concentration. So intent was he on his task that he hardly acknowledged our presence. We were hungry and tired. I felt as if my stomach housed tiny creatures gnawing at my innards. Tonde must have felt the same because he just threw down the hoe he was carrying and hurried straight to the kitchen. After a short moment, he stormed out of the kitchen, charged at Tapiwa, and punched him hard, squarely, in the face. The punch caught him off guard and landed on his nose which spurted blood on the sandy soil. He yelped and fell off his stool. Tonde was at an advantage; he must have thrown two more punches before what was happening finally dawned on Tapiwa. We were all astounded. Neither Tariro nor I knew what was happening but we stood by, relishing this moment in which Tapiwa was crying out for help, his nose a bloody mess. So, the almighty was actually vulnerable!

'*Chiiko*? What kind of fighting is this? Do you want to kill each other?' Gogo crossed the compound in quick, determined steps and hurriedly pulled them apart. She had stalled on the road, talking with the neighbour, as we headed home, so was not around when the fight started. 'You should be ashamed of yourselves. You are brothers and shouldn't be fighting like you want to draw blood.'

'What happened?' Tariro finally asked now that the best part was over. I knew we would be talking about this fight for quite some time. In Tapiwa's absence, of course.

'Go into the kitchen and see,' Tonde thundered. He was at his most boisterous. Our gentle Tonde. Of us all, he was the one most like Mother, and to see him behaving like Father was disturbing. Only Tapiwa seemed predisposed to violence; he had a natural proclivity for troublemaking.

We all turned to go to the kitchen as though directed by an

invisible force. I quickly saw what the problem was. The hearth was cold and clean. No fire had been made which meant that no food had been cooked. Tapiwa had failed at the one thing he was supposed to do. As if waking up late was not reason enough for us to hate him, he had also chosen not to cook for the peasants.

Have you ever heard of the snowball effect? The accumulation of many seemingly inconsequential factors into one humongous suffocating reason? Maybe this is easily explained in terms of nuance and complexity. I am sure the more learned among you have heard about this. Forgive the fancy language, but I am sure you have experienced these phenomena. We all have. The fallout between Tonde and Tapiwa wasn't clear cut. It was not a single event; it was gradual. Layers and layers of discontent and hatred accrued and calcified Tonde's heart, curdling whatever little emotion he had left for Tapiwa. We should have seen it coming. We should have tried hard to stop it. Perhaps we did see it, but we chose to ignore the signs. Perhaps we thought that not acknowledging the problem would make it disappear. How wrong we were! What started as a small issue set stage for the catastrophe that followed. This flicker of hatred culminated into unprecedented calamity.

Look at me trying to be the judge and jury in a story that I play more than just a passive role in. I am as much to blame as any of my siblings and parents, but enough of that. Let me continue with my narration.

The relationship between Tapiwa and Tonde was never restored; it seemed they were wary of each other. In the township, this was odd for young children, particularly siblings. This was not their first fight. Their fighting was habitual, some fiercer than others, but they almost always reconciled in a few hours. This particular year though, something different had happened. The delicate balance around which their relationship revolved was upset. Tapiwa distanced himself even more. He still woke up after we had all gone to till the unyielding land that was Gogo's field. He still pretended to study, but Tonde's fists had been worth something: he resumed with cooking duties. Tonde, however, stopped eating. He would just raid the nearby bush for *hacha*, a sweet wild fruit mainly eaten by donkeys. He would eat nothing but hacha and guzzle litres of water waiting for the evening meal. At first, Gogo was unfazed by this, waving it off as Tonde's 'mutinous' behaviour.

'Leave him be,' she would say, pursing her thin lips into a childish pout. 'If he chooses to starve himself then let him.'

Unlike Gogo, I was concerned, and I tried to coax him into eating. I coaxed and cajoled. I even cried. I tried to make him eat, but he would not be moved. He was adamant. He whispered, in confidence, 'I know Tapiwa is trying to poison my food, so I will not eat what he cooks.'

The seed of distrust had been sown, birthing a hatred that lasted longer than usual. I did not grasp the enormity or direness of this situation. I was too young.

Gogo weakened her resolve when Tonde began to lose weight. At the start of the holidays, he had been his usual plump self, with that roundness considered healthy in children, but now, his shoulder blades jutted out. Gogo pleaded with Tonde and Tapiwa to resolve 'this foolishness' between them. When neither brother yielded, Gogo settled to cooking herself. She would wake up earlier than usual, at dawn, and prepare food before we left. Tapiwa slept still, and we saw less and less of him, but we assumed he now spent long hours at Mukwadzi River with his newly found friends—the rowdy sort he wouldn't normally have associated with. Tonde became more and more cocooned. He withdrew into himself. The situation became direr so that by the time it was Christmas and Mother and Father had come to join us, there was hardly any civil word that passed between the two. Amid the merriment of Christmas festivities, Tonde was wallowing, sitting alone under the mango tree in a gloomy mood as though in mourning. As we danced to the popular rhumba tunes of Kanda Bongo Man's 'Billi', Tonde was nowhere to be found. He had chosen to have a lonely Christmas in the nearby bushes.

In some respects, the new year brought with it a sense of family and togetherness. We sat together, my brothers and I, under the mupfuti tree just behind the *hozi*, drinking cold and delicious Fanta. Tapiwa might have been withdrawn, but at least, he was there. Our parents had gone with Gogo to the community meeting. We sat, weighed down by the food we had eaten; it was a new year, we had over-indulged. It was then that we heard the maniacal laughter. It was demonic, otherworldly, and sent shivers down my spine. Tapiwa jerked, I spilt half my Fanta, and we all tried, desperately, to find the person laughing. The laughter halted as suddenly as it had started.

'Two brothers from the same womb at each other's throat, *imi ka!* The older will be killed by the younger, but it is the youngest who will bury both.' Then the disembodied voice broke into a sickening laugh. I was terrified; we all were. I remained rooted to the spot, albeit a second too long, for Tapiwa rose, abruptly, and followed the voice. When I finally gathered my wits and followed, Tapiwa and Tonde were already standing still, their backs rigid, having located the source of the chilling prediction.

It was none other than Brito. He sat leaning on the chicken coop, his legs wide open that we could see his large, semi-erect penis dipped in the soil. It had crusty smears of semen.

'So, Tonde is going to kill me.' It was Tapiwa's calmness as he said this terrible thing that unnerved me.

'Y-y-you surely c-can't believe this *mukoma*,' Tonde stuttered. I could tell he was terrified.

At this, Brito burst into deep laughter; he had brilliantly white teeth, it was disconcerting. On and on Brito laughed until fat drops of tears rolled down his gaunt face. We were surprised.

'One will die at the hand of the other, and the youngest will bury you both,' he repeated, in an ominously solemn voice. This sudden switch from laughter to solemnity was even more terrifying.

I was both angry and frightened by this unwelcome prediction by Brito. Angry because my brothers had just started to be civil toward each other and now that would be lost, again. Frightened because I knew very well that Brito was an esteemed fortune teller. I picked up a stone on impulse and hurled it at Brito. It hit him on his chest. It was a small stone, hurled in childish rage, and I swear it couldn't have hurt him in any way, but he howled and was set to launch himself at me.

Everything happened fast. Tonde hurled a brick at Brito, and it hit him on the head. As Brito fell backwards with a yelp of pain, Tapiwa slapped Tonde across the face, and the two started to fight. I stood, transfixed. I could have run for help, but I didn't. I could have done something, anything, to pull them apart, but I didn't. There was a sudden, haunting silence. Brito had stopped howling; he now lay still in a pool of blood. My heart hammered furiously in my chest. We all stood by Brito's seeming lifeless body, Tonde with a bloodied lip and Tapiwa with a swollen eye. Tonde moved closer to check if Brito had truly died because his breathing was imperceptible from where we stood. As he lowered himself, Brito lunged at him and began to choke him with all his might. They rolled, wrestling each other in the sandy soil. Brito was on top, Tonde at the bottom; Tonde was on top, Brito at the bottom. On and on they went. I didn't see Tapiwa pick up the brick, but I saw it rush past my face, and I closed my eyes tight. I heard a sickening and wet thump as the brick met with flesh. There was ringing silence. No one talked. No one moved. When I finally opened my eyes, Tonde lay lifeless, his eyes blank, staring but not seeing. I don't know if Tapiwa had missed Brito or had intended to kill Tonde before the latter had a chance to kill him as Brito predicted.

Brito laughed one last time—the same unsettling laughter—and yelled 'Tapiwa' before slipping into unconsciousness. All this time, I stood transfixed and didn't realize, until much later—after Tonde and Brito had been taken to the mortuary and Tapiwa had been cuffed and taken to the police—that I had shat my pants.

When I finally saw my brother, looking saintly in his prison-issue clothes, he was not himself. He didn't respond to any of my questions, but he laughed a lot, peals of unsettling laughter that was disturbingly similar to Brito's.

TO THE SON OF MY FRIEND
Ngansop Roy

No matter how much water I splashed against my arms and feet, the voices said my hands would never be clean. They were loud. They were right. There was wailing. I was awake but didn't step outside. It was dark outside. I looked forward to daybreak. It was empty inside. And noisy. I looked forward to seeing you safe and sound. I muttered prayers while counting the beads on the chain and only mounted my bicycle when the sun had scared the moon away. I rode out of the Mission's yard. The trails of blood, dyeing dewed grass on the neighbouring lawns, made me work the pedals faster. A few metres to the village centre, mothers wailed from within the first compounds. My legs didn't stop. They wouldn't even if I requested, until I reached your house, the fifth compound on the right, the one beside the butcher's shop.

I jumped off the bicycle so fast that my cassock got caught around the seat. I pulled it off and rushed to your bamboo fence. No woman screamed from there. The only litter in your front yard were *contri* fowl poop and leaves from neighbouring trees. The cock crowed. My eyes avoided the two tombs in the right corner of your compound, as usual. I touched my forehead, my shoulders and my chest. And when the door of the main house opened, when you stepped out with a broom, yawned, and scratched the area between your legs, I heaved a sigh and ran away. Did you notice me?

I rode back to the entrance of the village centre and leaned my bicycle on the tall grass beside the very first compound. A dry raffia palm helped me secure it there before I moved towards the keening. Trekking across the village, I stopped at every compound that hosted sad voices. And although sneering women dashed out of mourning houses upon my arrival, although those who remained didn't pay me any attention, I didn't retire until the lone road contouring the village brought me back to the two-wheeler. If only one villager cared for my presence, then I had a purpose.

Should you have visited the afflicted compounds to show your face already, you would have noticed that the ceilings of the mud houses in their front yards were shattered. When I walked in this morning, the corn grains that fell from there served the contri fowls' early breakfast. Their bamboo fences were broken, if not half burnt. 'May we find comfort in *Cyepɔ*,' I said to every household. I always used we and not you, even for pains alien to a man. Patting shoulders and caressing wet jaws gave meaning to my hands. If a child cried unattended, I picked it up and sang beautiful psalms until it quiesced.

Although they rarely spoke, the girls who sat in foetal position in the corners of their rooms commanded more of my attention. Where their mothers permitted, I walked in and sat on the bare floor by their side. My hands grabbed their fingers and gathered a chain of beads into their palms. I muttered the pleas without caring if they said them along. I never asked them to stop crying. Instead, my head fell towards my knees so no one could notice the tears streaming down my own face.

On my ride back to the Mission, the voices corrupted the birdsong. I heard the voice of the woman who said she didn't need a cutlass with two sides to wipe her daughter's tears. The voice of the *ntui-ntui* who asked if my cassock was not too tight. The voice of my friend, sobbing and moaning. The voice of my mother begging me to not leave her alone. The growling voice of the man who licked the ground, raised his index finger, and spoke the fate, to the third and fourth generations, of every ntui-ntui. The voice of the woman who looked at me with swollen eyes and asked when Cyepô would come. When their voices died out, I was rolling back and forth beside my bicycle, wrestling alone in the grass, slapping the trails of blood, and repeating that everyone will find comfort in Cyepô.

I was seven when I first heard the word ntui-ntui. I had two playmates: Tamo, the now village blacksmith, and a smart girl whom I want you to know was my friend, our good friend. While playing at the market, we had picked two plums on a counter without handing a coin. The seller shouted ntui-ntui. Before the panic could spread, my mother shot the seller with their plums and pulled us three to her counter.

Unlike Tamo and my friend, I lived with my mother only. I watched her do the farming and the harvest, fetch the wood and use the axe, bring the food and make the soup. She only sold at the market sometimes to pay my school fees to the Mission. Her produce alone loaded our barns and filled our stomachs, and there was yet enough left to gift to needy neighbours. So when the village boys said that their uncles wanted to give her coins to sleep at our house, I said she didn't need their money.

We never lacked. But I sometimes wondered about my father. Did you ever wonder about your father, too? I couldn't tell what about my father my heart was longing to know. Or what he would do if he ever came home and started living with us. I thought about the likelihood but never asked. And my mother never mentioned him either.

I was twelve the second time I heard the word ntui-ntui. It was during the food crisis. Sky and earth had gone dry for months, and Cyepɔ seemed deaf to our pleas. Villagers gathered around my mother's bamboo fence in the evenings. And when she let them into our compound, the first compound, they rushed near our barn to scramble for what she could offer.

On one of such evenings, after everyone had left, after we had closed the fence, shut the door of the mud house in the yard, and locked ourselves up in the main house to rest, I heard loud noises outside. I elbowed my mother out of her sleep. She grabbed me and asked that I hold my breath and lay still. I did as she bade.

The following morning, our already starving village saddened more. Those with loaded barns like my mother saw their reserves reduced. Mothers dangled their arms and screamed the names of their sons. Teenage girls stooped in the corners of their houses, and strangers visited them in rows as though they were widows. Grieving families screamed ntui-ntui alongside curses, and people who came to show their faces clapped their hands in bewilderment. I trekked with Tamo and my friend to show my face at every afflicted compound too. Dark clouds swept over our village for days. My mother knelt in her yard, beside the last corn grains that fell from the ceiling like raindrops. She looked to the sky and asked Cyepɔ to let the hands that filled the barns refill them. And on the third day of mourning, the skies wept water on all that she had sown.

I was eighteen the third time I heard the word ntui-ntui. The space between my legs had started changing. My mother trusted me enough to let me return home alone after sunset. That night, before I reached the fence of the first compound, a stranger said a warrior wanted to see me. I called him a fool and walked away. But before we turned off the candlelight to close our eyes, someone broke into our house. He was mature, well-built, and shabby. He had a bare and hairy chest, a loincloth wrapped around his waist and laps, and rings of brown beads hanging halfway from his knees down to his ankles. Both sides of the cutlass in his hand glistened. He held it out in the middle of our bed when my mother tried to grab me. She screamed ntui-ntui at the top of her voice. But no one came to help. Not even those whose baskets were filled from her barns. The man asked me not to look back while he pulled me out. But I did. I saw my mother screaming that I shouldn't leave her alone.

I spent days with men I had never met, strange people. Their filthy camp and their habit of resolving everything through a fight only fuelled my longing to escape. But all attempts to return to the village failed. First, they called me 'son of a warrior', and then, once, the man, who had snatched me from the bosom of my mother and showed me how to wield the two-sided cutlass, called me a warrior. He taught me that respect was taken, not given, and honour and pleasures were deserved by those who devoted their lives to protecting their people. From hygiene to language, I hated their ways. But after months of exercise and shrinking, I surrendered to the taste of bushmeat and onions.

I rubbed my right knee in dust and pledged respect to the man whose presence only ever filled me with resentment. If all the battles I fought against neighbouring invaders protected our village, then somehow, I was fighting to protect my mother too. I stood by his side and followed his orders. Our village was untouchable from outside. He turned me into that thing. Wait. No. I let him do it. I did.

And then one night, he said the time had come to visit the village centre. I hoped it was operation empty-their-barns. I hoped to see my mother once again. And maybe, somehow, find a way to escape. But there was no looting, no commotion. It was just him, his two-sided cutlass, and me. He took me to the spot where he claimed to have worked as a butcher before he turned eighteen, before he was snatched from the bosom of his mother. He smiled when he said that someday my son would turn eighteen too, that someday I would have to pass on my legacy. I didn't have a son, but I smiled too.

Then he broke into the fifth compound on the right. He threatened to shed blood if anyone screamed. He brandished his two-sided cutlass and called the father of the house a woman for not having one. The mother touched her forehead, her shoulders, and her chest in cycles and shushed. I knew that household. They knew me too. The teenage girl looked at me with fear on her face. The retired butcher asked her to lay naked before ordering me to take my honour. And when I felt his blade on my neck, I didn't do what my mother would have bid.

After visiting the village this morning, it dawned on me that last night was my darkest. My last indeed, I pledge. Upon return to my room at the Mission, I wrapped my blood-stained cassock in plastic and put it in my bag, right above two cutlasses. I was heading to the parish priest's office when one of the Mission boys informed me that the priest would like to see me after the service. I had wanted to see him before it, but his word prevailed.

My feet would not let me walk to my assigned seat beside the Mission boys at the altar. I wiped the front bench on the side of the assembly and sat there instead. My friend was not yet there. Most villagers preferred the benches at the back, but not my friend. I monitored the entrance and waited to see if perhaps after so many years, she wouldn't bother starting something new, sharing the bench. Tamo was seated at the back with his wife and daughter, avoiding my eyes in public as usual. The service was about to begin when you walked in with my friend. You wrapped your arm around her shoulder and held her fingers like I held those of the teenage girls seated in their rooms this morning. You both moved forward to sit alone on the front bench as you had always done. But upon noticing me there, my friend drifted to the next bench without letting her eyes meet mine.

Whenever you looked at me, I looked away. The voices asked me to. I didn't make the sign of peace. I didn't walk to the aisle to eat altar bread. I had stopped eating bread on the seventh day. I nodded every time the parish priest spoke consoling words to afflicted families. I said 'amen' when he said it was the way of everyone. But when he called Cyepɔ 'the Son of Man', the voices went wild. They screamed 'son of woman', instead. They said I should make no such claim. They dared me to say your name. Toukap maybe, like my friend's father? Momo maybe, like my friend's paternal grandfather? Perhaps Fotso, like her maternal grandfather? They cited many names, but not Djoko. All possible names, except mine. What is your name? When the priest said everyone should expect His return, the voices said that I had always been expecting in vain.

I didn't wait for the service to end. I lurched out to beat my skull in the corridor, and once the priest announced that the Mission's coffers had been broken into overnight, I rushed to wait at the door of his office.

It was Tamo who first gave me the news. He said 'our friend has changed' as though I was still young and innocent. He said that whenever my friend stepped out of the house, the village boys asked her how many coins their uncles had offered her, that her mother was begging random men, young and old, single or married, to take her without any rites.

Tamo said these things on one of those days when I escaped the ntui-ntui camp to sleep around the Mission. My trainer had stopped questioning my movements. Although I had shed tears in what he called a moment of glory, he claimed I had proven my worth in his eyes. Which worth? Every dusk reminded me of my soullessness, and the space within me had started filling with voices. The very day he had granted me permission to wander out of the camp at will, I had returned to the village and found my mother's compound crowded with tall grass. Tamo said she had left the village without a word. I had returned to the camp with more tears. And had made it a habit to sleep on the lawns beside the Mission every seventh night.

The news about my friend brought a strange feeling. It was sad, but not like the disappearance of my mother. First there was a tiny leap in my chest, and then heavy drumming that made me sweat at every thought of her. Was it a girl or a boy? I wondered if they would look like me. What will happen to them at eighteen? The prospects looked shady in either case. I commissioned Tamo. For lack of riches, I proposed to build my friend's father a bamboo fence so tall no one could scale it before the occupants could brace themselves or escape. I proposed to build her mother a barn as big as my mother's. I proposed to do everything my mother had told me to do the day a woman agreed to grant me a descendant.

Tamo agreed to help. He would do everything to bring me back to the village. He had started making iron utensils for the Mission. He would help me convince our friend's parents to let a ntui-ntui take their daughter. And I would return to the village to beat hot iron with him, if not farm for a living. He was ready to attest that I was only a good warrior, that I had never brought my two-sided cutlass into the village.

The day Tamo returned with their response, I had showered twice, and not eaten any onions, just in case they wanted to meet me. He gave me a stern look and two solid blows. I fell on my back. My lips bled. 'You fool, she was our friend,' he said. He said our friend's father had punched him too. Her mother had pronounced curses but had later called her daughter behind the house to say that we were once friends and that maybe her daughter would prefer being with me than ending like my mother. I didn't know how to process that. I spat blood and asked Tamo what our friend had said herself. He told me she had threatened to wash out her bowels with *zoazoa* if anyone let me around her.

Tamo said if I had told him myself, he would have punched me once, only. He didn't speak to me for days, then months. He didn't come to meet me anymore. He would bring his utensils to the Mission by day and escape before the sun shied away. I wanted to be of help to my friend. I felt bad that I couldn't show her my contrition. I wandered into the village a few times. I cleaned the first compound at night and escaped before daytime. And the day I saw the village boys laughing beside her compound, I felt bad that my pain was not any close to hers. The voices started ringing, and every minute spent in the village only made them louder. Every night spent at the camp made me burn with fury at the man who had made me who I was. No, he didn't make me do it, did he? I did it. That is what the voices said. So, I cut myself off and settled in the shrubs around the Mission.

The night the parish priest met me wrestling alone on the lawn and asked what my soul was longing for, I said comfort. I told him I had wielded a cutlass on battlefields. His eyelids fluttered. I said I had snatched my honour by ripping my friend of hers. He didn't recognize the young man who had schooled at the Mission for years. I didn't know how else to let him see me. When I professed being the son of the woman with the biggest barns in the village, he took me in and helped me clean up. He said I could find comfort in Cyepô. I told him my friend had refused to see me as the father. He said I could become a new man, a father of many, a man with clean hands and honour, who stands behind the altar and harbours so much comfort that it spills over to his children. But I would have to wait until you were eighteen, until you were able to stand alone.

I joined the boys who cleaned the Mission and toured the village to announce the Good News. The parish priest told me what to say and taught me how to say it. The day he branded me as the proof of Cyepô's clemency, he gave me a cassock and a bicycle. I told the villagers that Cyepô would come to save them. If it was true for them, it could be true for me too, I hoped. The voices did not always agree. But I screamed this Good News while riding along the dusty paths. I entered wherever I was welcomed. But at the fifth compound on the right, I only ever peeped above the fence.

After I joined the Mission, my friend's parents stopped coming to the service every seventh day. Several villagers too. My friend didn't come until thirty-five market days had passed. The day I saw her with a wrapped cloth in her arms, she was a woman already. She always sat ahead of the assembly and listened attentively to the teachings. If I stood beside the parish priest while he shared altar bread, she wouldn't walk to the aisle. She never replied to my letters. The one time I dared to walk to her, Tamo threatened to deform my face. I stood like a pillar outside your compound the day her parents, your grandparents, were laid to rest. I watched you grow from her arms to your two legs. I watched you run around the village and sprout into a teenager. The day Tamo said you had ears as large and shoulders as broad as mine, I spent the night looking at myself in the mirror. I would gather the coins the parish priest gave me into an envelope and send the Mission boys to drop it at your compound, but every seventh day, the same envelope would be returned, yet veiled, in the offering basket.

Unable to approach you, I found comfort in watching you blossom from a distance. Perhaps you didn't need me anyway. I settled for this, hoping that someday I could become the new man who would stand behind the altar, whose comfort in Cyepô would be so much that it would spill over to those around. Perhaps it would spill over to you, too. And to my friend. The parish priest said I was doing well. I believed him. I hushed the voices. Until last night.

In his office, I bowed before the parish priest and waited for him to offer me a seat. I scrutinized his face for traces of fury. But his stare was blank. He gathered a bunch of papers and beckoned me to sit. I babbled when he asked what the purpose of my life was. First, I said it was to protect the village. Then I said it was to cater to the needs of forsaken children. And when he began to shake his head, I said it was to bring comfort with the Good News.

Before asking another question, he cautioned me to breathe in and choose my words wisely. He reminded me of how low I was when he picked me up from the ground. The voices said that his use of past tense wasn't fitting, that it made it seem like something had improved. He spoke of the promise Cyepô had made to me through him: that I could be a new man if only I would wait until I was ready. He said you were old enough to be a man, and I could finally tender my application to holy order. But first, he wanted to know what happened before daybreak.

There were only voices in my cupboard, no bones. I said I had wanted to meet him before the service. I told him that a ntui-ntui had visited my room at the Mission. That he had pulled on the cincture around my black robe and said it didn't fit. That he had told me no man could renounce the two-sided cutlass. That this ntui-ntui had thrown my cutlass to me and said only I could perform my duty, only I could snatch you from my friend and teach you how to wield a cutlass.

'But you are still here,' the priest said. 'I am proud of you.'

He sipped a glass of water as though to help push down all what I had declared. Then he called a Mission boy to bring in envelopes. He placed them on the table before me.

'Our coffers are empty. I cannot trust you unless you say everything,' he said.

The envelopes contained all the notes I had sent to my friend, but no coins. I explained that all the money I sent to her compound came from what he gave me as my periodic allowance, and that, if asked, my friend would attest that this money always returned to the coffers, anyway. And then I confessed that it was the visiting ntui-ntui who helped himself to the coffers before exiting the Mission that night.

The priest looked me in the eyes and said he believed me. But the villagers screaming in the corridors that a ntui-ntui could only bring ill news to the Mission reminded me that the priest's trust alone was not enough. I leaned my head towards my knees and hit my skull twice.

'Bless me, father,' I said in a breathy voice, 'I am not worthy.'

'Cyepɔ has long forgiven you,' he said.

I fell to his feet and said my hands were not clean. I told him I had followed the ntui-ntui to the village before daybreak. That they were many more at the village centre. That I had not intervened while they emptied women's barns. That I had not protected the teenage girls. That I had waited for most of them to run away with loaded arms, and at the fifth compound on the right, I had wielded my cutlass to take the breath of the man who came to see me perform my alleged duty. That I had run unclean into my room at the Mission and only returned to the village by morning to comfort afflicted families.

'Turn from your ways and find comfort in the Son of Man,' he said.

At the sound of 'Son of Man', the voices hit the corners of my head. 'He is the son of a woman,' I screamed, and wrestled on the carpet. 'He is not mine.'

'You can only be a new man after you pardon yourself.'

'Their voices say it, I am nothing,' I said. 'She has not pardoned me. Those men will not pardon me either. When their cutlasses come, I will be the cause of more grief.'

'What will you have me do, then?'

'Bless me, father.'

After he placed his hands on my head and wished me well, I lifted my bag to my shoulder. Ignoring the sneering women outside the Mission while mounting my bicycle was a struggle. I left without disclosing that after taking the breath of the ntui-ntui who visited me last night, I dragged him on the grass and laid him to rest where I once came to sleep at night. Was it worth mentioning that he was my father? I never called him so. But the voices say you deserve to know.

When I rode past the forge, Tamo said I was a fool for leaving without looking at your eyes and telling you who I really was inside my chest. He didn't say it exactly so. He beckoned to the fifth compound on the right and said his dissuasive blows must have weakened me over the years. His voice added to the loud voices, so I u-turned. But my friend's grip of you, her uncompromising stare when I neared the entrance of your bamboo fence, reminded me why I could never get to you. And so, I sit here, putting sentences together to tell you about a man you may never meet nor understand. Grabbing you in my arms would have said what these words can't say. Perhaps you would have felt or filled the space in my chest. Perhaps you would have heard and hushed the voices in me. But my friend's decision is paramount.

I will drop this note at the forge and leave, hoping it gets to you. Run to my friend's side after reading this account. Maybe she will brush through these lines with you. Perhaps she will use different words to say who I am when you ask her. Believe her. Wrap your arm around her shoulders like you know too well. Grab her hand and while fidgeting with her fingers, whisper in her ear that you will never leave her alone. If nothing else, I may find peace in the thought that this is a legacy.

I will cycle away from the village, hoping to do the same, hoping to find her, hoping to return to the one thing I know how to be: the son of my mother.

BROWN EYES
Charles Muhumuza

I

'Brown eyes?'

'Yes. A rich, thick, dark, coffee brown.'

'You do understand what this is, John.'

'Yes. But you know I've always been a romantic. A classical beauty, can't you see it?'

Dora paces, a measured distance between her steps. Her gaze hovers over everything in the room, but she does not look at me.

'If you want people thinking our daughter is dark-eyed why not have it inscribed on her forehead, yeah?' she says, still holding out her gaze.

'Okay, Dora. What do you think?' I ask.

'Violet, with a sharp strain of yellow,' she replies, looking at me now.

'How about a plain light violet?'

'Sure. With a trace of yellow.' She smiles. I return the smile.

It's not often that we fight, but when it has to do with family politics, no less is expected. I often bait her into arguments, but it usually turns into a lesson on science or society, concluded by a joke about the teacher being taught.

She's a doctor, a genome editor with a private practice in the townships that she took over after her father's passing. The ethics regarding the use of the tool forbid her from working on our daughter, but I don't think she would go beyond the rules even if parents could edit.

We didn't originally plan on having any children. Dora has always felt that her work on improving the human race is beyond the domestic activity of child-rearing and that my work as a teacher in the townships should satisfy that instinct.

It was my idea to expand our family, and after some consideration, Dora compromised.

I thought maybe after having a child I'd start to see Kwezi differently.

They say our children are miracles. It is humanity edging closer to perfection and fulfilled potential. To me, the township children are the true miracles. How quickly they learn, much faster than the politicians make us believe. I believe the best of them would be able to compete in our environment. I think they are made out to be much worse than they actually are. The picture of life outside the community is painted way too grim for its citizens.

The first time I crossed the wall was as a policymaker, seven years ago. We had been fed tales of wildness, of a people susceptible to disease and sickness. They never told us it was a beautiful wildness, nature so un-curated, a people joyful in a world of so little. We had gone to make a new proposal to the elders of the townships: a provision of services in exchange for the labour they provide for the different projects that power the community.

My colleagues decried the wildness, the subhuman conditions, and toasted to the success we had achieved. What I noticed was a remarkable beauty. A thousand children with brown eyes everywhere you turned. A different strangeness from what we had inside the community. It's hard to imagine that the East Africa I know was once made up of such eyes.

Our daughter arrives. We name her Eva. Her eyes are light violet with a hidden trace of yellow that sharpens in the light. A thrilling contrast to her dark skin. Her little fingers are so thin. You can already tell they are her mother's.

'Why didn't you tell me the township was such a beautiful place?'
    'Striking, John, but not beautiful.'
    'The children. They are so eager, so bright.'
    'Thought of advocating for favourable policies for them, to begin with?' Dora asks me.
    'The teaching is definitely helping. You can see it in their eyes,' I tell her.
    She looks at me and smiles. The kind of smile that means she asked you a question, and answered it herself, all without saying a word.
    Sometimes I think she is too logical; her father definitely tweaked something extra in her.

I started my teaching career in the townships, three years ago. The townships are mostly inhabited by people whose parents or grandparents couldn't afford to have their children's genome edited to remove disease-laden DNA, and so couldn't dictate strains that could make them more competitive. Some were prevented by religion or belief from accessing the services, and many still held those beliefs.

The townships, scattered outside the borders of the cities, are considered part of East Africa but not the community. We have a responsibility towards them, so we provide education and health services. The health services inside the community are covered by the state. Dora has been running her private health programme in the townships for about ten years.

'How was Eva today?' I ask Dora, as I cradle Eva in my arms.

'She blows my mind away. Always doing something I thought she was too young to do,' Dora tells me.

I laugh.

'You should spend more time with her. So far, the hours you've spent with her are below the parental requirement,' she adds.

'I should. I should. To think she'll be solving humanity's problems in a year,' I reply.

Dora laughs.

He looks at me. Sharp brown eyes tearing into me. They seem to tell a thousand stories all at once.

I find comfort in the classrooms. There is a certain chaotic order I crave. The presence of the students, the large glass windows, the wild trees outside. There is a certain joy that comes with witnessing a realization of knowledge. How the eyes light up when they figure something out. No one does this better than Kwezi. His little eyes light up in amazement at solving a problem.

I catch myself questioning Eva, seeking to see a flick of his hand in hers or the left-bending smirk of his on her lips as she begins to laugh. Sometimes she gives me what I'm looking for.

'I find the townships so fascinating,' I tell Dora.

'They are, in their own way.'

'Not in their own way, just honest.'

'Honest to the community's deception?'

'No, Dora, something. I can't explain it.'

'They don't like people like you.'

'You speak so little of them, yet you've known them so deeply.'

I rush my speech and regret it. I can speak of the townships. I can speak of Dora. But to speak of townships and Dora is to speak of her father. She keeps his memories to herself and the programme as a little kindness to his memory. I met him briefly. The day I met her. A celebrated genome editor who had chosen to make the townships his home. He had come as a visiting professor giving his inaugural lecture at the university. All my friends went, but science has never interested me. I was moving around the campus when I saw her. There was an amazement in her eyes. In a place where eyes are as unique as ears or thumbprints, hers spoke a different language altogether.

It was three months of wildness. Three months of abandoning thought. Three months that I can say changed my life. She suddenly left with her father before the end of the semester. I never saw that Dora again.

It's like Kwezi's little eyes know nothing but sadness. Even when he smiles or laughs, you can see the sadness linger. I want to get a little happiness and put it in them.

His brown eyes haunt me. Sometimes I feel I've known him more deeply before. In a past life.

Dora worries. She thinks I'm unwell. She says she has seen it before in her father. The mind wandering. In the days that led to him trying to burn down his programme building.

I think it's different. I would never do the things he did even if I wanted to. She once told me about them. She says it started the day they left the university. He swore never to return to the community. He thought we had lost track of the use of science and

174

the tool, disappointed in what was the growing focus of scientists. He thought the powers of editors should be curbed. But that wasn't the madness. The madness was when he tried un-editing DNA, re-implanting that which he thought was the true human identity, the uncorrupted human condition.

'I want him here.'

'Who?' Dora asks me.

'Kwezi,' I tell her.

'Who's Kwezi?'

'You should see him. You should know him.'

'Don't do this,' Dora tells me, her voice almost broken.

I tell her that I need him here. The possibility of this place as his home. I want her to give him a chance, to understand how it feels.

'You can't keep doing this to me.' I can tell she is frustrated.

'John, your hours with Eva are failing. What makes you think we can afford to take care of any more children.'

'Trust me, please,' I plead. 'He needs us.'

'So do thousands, millions of those children. You think you care more than I do? You think you know more about their suffering than I do?' Dora asks me.

'My life changed because of those children,' she sighs. 'You ever wondered why I didn't want to have children? You wonder why I hate my father? Have you ever questioned why we left the university so suddenly? It was because of you, John. He despised you. He despised everyone in the community with your misplaced obsessions. He despised himself. He would never let me have my child with someone like you. He thought he could rewrite everything.'

It feels like my life, our life, is being swept up by a flood. I want to ask questions, but instead, I pull her closer to me as she cries.

She pulls away and pats her eyes.

'We have Eva. I don't think they can allow us an adoption. Maybe we should look at a three-way. It could make things easier. I can find the third parent,' she says at last.

'Sure about this?' I ask, and she nods, in the curtly way of settled matters.

'But there won't be need for the verifications,' I tell her.

'Why?'

'All I need is your permission and the elders' acceptance,' I reply. 'I have the permits.'

When I make it to the townships, I'm led to a large brown hall surrounded by huge trees. I find it intimidating, and I think this is its purpose. The elders are intimidating too. Old men and women dressed in their traditional garbs. I show them the documents.

They introduce themselves and ask what brings me. I introduce myself and tell them I want to take care of a son of theirs. Dora told me to avoid words like 'adopt' and to show reverence. They tell me this is the home of their sons. This is what they were made for. I tell them this will always be home to him. They talk among themselves.

A light-skinned man, who seems a little too young to be on the council, asks me who it is I want to take care of.

'Kwezi,' I tell him.

He is about to say something, but the others start talking. Some laugh.

'That won't be possible,' their leader says. You can tell by her dress and the way the others venerate her that she's the leader.

They all keep quiet for a while.

'All these children are sons of the land. Daughters of the townships. But for some, Kwezi and a few others, this is more than home to them. These are children that the good doctor refused to adulterate. And he brought them here, told us to take care of them before your enforcers swooped in and crucified him on our own land. His own land. So, Mr John, understand why we can't let them go.'

I feel a tinge of coldness crawl upon me.

'The good doctor was my father,' I say.

I should say father as they would but can't bring myself to lie so blatantly, taking advantage of their culture and language.

'Father-in-law,' I quickly add.

The elders ask for my documents again.

I hand them to the leader.

They pass them around.

'How do you know Kwezi?' the light-skinned man asks.

'I'm his history teacher. I think he has a lot of potential,' I reply.

'That young boy never forgets a single thing. Nothing. Very intelligent. But you must know that all our children have potential,' he replies. I can feel the contempt in his voice.

The elders speak to each other.

'We do not trust you people, and we cannot pretend to,' the leader says, her eyes fixed on me.

I want to tell her we are one people, one East Africa. I do not know what she expects me to reply.

'We however do feel that the way you've carried out your profession in this home of ours is commendable. One can say it's your home too now.' She smiles.

They all nod.

'We should give him a name,' one says.

They laugh.

'If the students haven't given him one already,' another man who seemed uninterested in the proceedings says, laughing with his mouth wide open.

They all burst out in laughter, and I join them.

II

I'm playing in the field when I'm summoned by the Wazee. My

friends tease me. I think it has to do with school. I'm a little nervous, but I know I haven't done anything wrong. It crosses my mind that it could be something good, but I doubt it.

I'm also nervous and excited that I'm entering the Great Hall for the first time.

The Great Hall is large. Amazingly large. The Wazee sit in a circle at the front of it, so there is a long way to walk if one comes in from the back as I have. Mr John sits in the circle too but stands out from the others. He isn't dressed as smartly, in flowing kanzus and kikoy. The roof of the Great Hall is high at the centre and descends at the sides such that they almost touch the ground. The roof looks suspended because it does not touch the walls. The walls are short and brown. I wonder how they built it, the Great Hall. The space between the roof and walls brings in a lot of air and a lot of light. It feels great to be here. I'm still a little nervous as to why they called me.

The chief of the Wazee greets me and asks my name. I know she knows it because she knows everyone in the township and even beyond. I tell her my name. She asks me if I know Mr John, and I say that I do, that he is my history mwalimu. I like Mr John. He loves when I answer questions, especially when I answer by asking. He laughs a bit and says something about me being smart and mutters 'potential' under his breath. He makes me want to be a teacher. But I think I should be a doctor.

The chief of the Wazee asks me if I'm happy here in the township, and I say yes. She tells me about the community and asks if I'd want to live there. I tell her I've always wanted to see it. I hear in the cities there are people whose eyes actually glow like the bugs in the fields at night. I really want to see what it is like there.

I'm embarrassed to admit it, but they laugh. The Wazee tell me that Mr John wants to take care of me, and I'm to go with him. I smile and thank them. And thank him.

I do not say goodbye to my friends. I'll be seeing them soon.

Mr John seems very happy. He tells me he is Baba now.

'Are you excited?' he asks me.

'Yes. I wonder what it's like there,' I tell him.

'Oh,' he laughs, 'you are going to see it. It's different. Just a little more developed.'

The Wazee have told us before that the community citizens only chose a different path; we are not less developed. Some Wazee say the community people forget that it is people like us that discovered CRISPR tools and all those machines that they use. That they are intentionally forgetting so as to rewrite our history. I would also say we created those people, but the Wazee say we are all forged by the will of a higher power. I think it's just them being hopeful; hope is the one thing we can't lose if we want a better world, they say. I do want a better world for us. I don't think we should have to fall sick or get aches or go to bed hungry. They tell us that the future rests with each one of us. I hope I can do something; I really hope. They tell us that we all have a role to play. They tell us many things.

I don't think excited is what I'm feeling. I know curiosity is not a feeling, but it's how I feel inside. I want to see how the community looks. How different it is from home.

The wall is a tunnel. Or maybe it's a wall with a tunnel in it. It's grey and long and full of electric lights. We make a few stops along the way.

We are here. I think it's beautiful. Mr John was right to say different. It's the buildings I notice first. They have a rhythm in the way they are built. In themselves and with each other. It's like they were built at the same time. Everything looks like a mathematical calculation. I don't think I've seen any birds, but they should be flying in pairs.

We go to Mr John's house. It feels like home from the moment you see it, but not home like the townships. Everything seems soft and comfortable, from the light blue walls to the green grass and flowers. I see her. She comes, and I see why. Why it felt this way.

Mama.

Maybe that's why it felt like home. I remember. Maybe that's why I cry. Her eyes do not show that they remember. I wonder how she can forget. But they cry. She calls me to her arms wide.

'You are perfect,' she tells me.

I wonder how she can forget. I thought the citizens remembered everything.

Mama takes me to Eva. She says Eva is my sister. She is a baby. Her eyes glow like I heard people's eyes do in the cities. But they are nice and not scary.

Baba takes me to school. He looks happy. The school is big. He tells me I can study until I become a doctor. The classroom is also very big. There are no windows. You cannot see outside. There are plenty of things inside. There is everything to play and study with. There are many mwalimus, and they teach us in small groups. They tell me to call them teacher. Other children come and look at me; their eyes have many colours. Green, yellow, even red. The teachers say everyone should welcome people into the community. That life is very hard outside. It's good for people to come; I want to play like them.

I miss my friends. Even after all this time, outside the house doesn't feel much like home.

Mama and Baba take us to the beach, Eva and me. It reminds me of how I used to play in the streams in the townships. It's a very beautiful place. Most of the beaches are closed to the community, as the leaders prefer the citizens swimming and playing in more controlled environments. Mama and Baba take us to a place by the shores of Lake Nalubaale. It's outside the community but without a township near it.

Eva wants us to build a small house in the sand. She goes too close to the water, and I worry that the house will be washed away by the waves, but I see her pick out rocks from the water. She is very smart.

'Let's draw an outline first,' I tell her.

'You can help do that,' she replies.

It must be the brightness of the sun. I see a reflection of my eyes in Eva's, a brown digging into violet as she giggles over something. Maybe her eyes have a brown in them too. I pass Eva a stone to start building. I look at mama, and she waves at us. She still doesn't know. But I see a beginning. The unfolding. This could be how it all starts.

TAFFETA
Queen Nneoma Kanu

An air balloon lighter than air was made from taffeta. It had been an experiment and it worked.

There are many things in my life that I do not know how they got there in the first place, like the status that my mansion in Lekki Peninsula has afforded me. The Lekki Peninsula is a haven for the high and mighty, with its expansive residential suburbia flanked on both sides by blocks of homes *furnished* with running water and electricity. In Lekki, you are adorned with an aura that throws poverty into the Atlantic Ocean. But am I safe in this new skin, in this pristine newness that surrounds me? My mother tried to prepare me for the life of abundance that I now live, but my mind tells me I remain in danger as long as I live in this skin that has turned me into prey.

I am still in my feelings about my new life when my doorbell sounds off from the hallway. I wait for the shrill of the doorbell to whistle again before uncurling myself from the sofa. On getting to the door, I put my weight on my toes, stretching out my neck to see through the glass panel of the oak door. The pampas grass in my hallway brushes my arm. The prickly sensation through my skin warns me to be on my guard. I take a deep breath, unlock the latch, and the door swings open. I step back to see that there is a boxed parcel on my doormat from Jumia. And a delivery man. His legs are spread apart close to the base of my flowerbed, and he keeps his eyes on me like a henchman from a mafia movie. The flesh on his face form perfect balls on both sides of his cheeks because he is smiling, and it looks like he is expecting me to smile back. But I cock my head to the side to look past his frozen smile and arresting steady gaze. Something tells me we might not be alone, with the way he is standing with confidence, not touching the parcel and watching my reaction from a safe distance.

His silhouette helps to block the ray of sunlight that is threatening to blind me, but I am more relieved that the policeman I started noticing across the street five days ago is not at his duty post. Each time I see him, hitting the soles of his boots on the concrete pavement or whistling or strolling past my house, the song 'Police Dey Come, Army Dey Come' plays in my head. It's from Fela's 'Sorrow, Tears and Blood.' I wonder if the policeman is watching me, if this cloud of newness I have acquired around me makes me stand out like sore on unblemished skin. I am sure my mind plays this game where everything around me is a signal, a warning. As I surrender myself to this life of new memories, the life I have lived for so long points its fingers at me, mocks me. There is this wavelength of communication going on in my head and crawling down my skin, but there's nothing to fear. Nothing will break my mind. My past is not here anymore; it can no longer play games with me.

My eyes return to the boxed parcel on the doormat, and the blown-up body of the dead journalist is in my head. They had watched him too. They had played games with him too. And then on his daughter's birthday, they sent the letter. He opened it at the breakfast table where he sat with his family and the bomb blew him into many red-fleshed pages, his body strewn all over the breakfast table. It was like his life never mattered.

The delivery man takes a step towards me, his arms stretched out as if to touch me. I stay frozen to the spot as he, instead, hands me an iPad for my signature.

'Thank you for choosing Jumia.' His face is still smiling, clearly part of his job. I give him another quick scan before collecting the iPad. He is wearing a green polo neck with the company logo, the hems of his jean trousers tucked into his black boots. I scrawl my signature across the device and leave a five-star review before returning it to him. He steps back, and I pick up the box, shutting the door behind me. I set the box on the glass table in the living room, my red *KISS* press-on toenails peeking back at me through the glass.

I take off the box lid. There is a note tucked inside the tissue-padded box: *Sent with all my love, to my beloved Lady, Raoul.*

I gently unfold the wrapping and underneath is an exquisite deluxe silk taffeta. I caress the smooth weave of the fabric and gasp, then I remember my nouveau habit with Raoul has come to stay. You see, I used to hustle the streets of Lagos during the lean years before I met Raoul, buying roadside *akara* wrapped in old newspapers when I was out of business, or attending international trade fairs on the arms of a moneyed man when I was back on the clock.

The night I met Raoul was no different from my usual nights of misfortunes. I was strolling down Allen for a packet of mosquito coil when Raoul's Range Rover pulled up beside me. He said he recognized me from somewhere he couldn't remember, but none of that mattered that night. All I wanted was to sink into the plush comfort of his car, so I got in. That same week, we flew to the trade summit at the Burj al Arab, where the animated speaker on the podium left me in awe as he clicked bright pictures on the projector screen and talked about the trade borders in the Middle East. The presenter gave a few minutes for Q&A, and I felt Raoul's warm hands teasing my thighs when I stood up to say I found it interesting that there were poor, ghettoed areas of Gaza and Yemen in the shadows of the rich moneyed areas of Qatar and the UAE.

After the summit, Raoul took my hands, and we strolled out of the hotel lobby. I decided to stay with him as soon as the rays from the sun hit our faces as we walked down the stairs. It felt unfamiliar that a man would talk to me as though I mattered. He never seemed to mind that I knew nothing about things he knew everything about—Kleinian principles, ataraxian philosophies, his name being patronymic. Of all the things he talked so passionately about, I loved two, the goddess Athena and the Mediterranean Sea. I adored the woman that Athena was—astute, calculated, creative, a daughter of potent gods. Athena gave me fond memories of my mother and helped me recapture the smoulder of affection between us that could have been but was not. Raoul's voice was soothing like the sea, and it lured me back to my life on the beach, when I woke up to the alluring song of the ocean and the warmth of the sands that pricked my naked feet. The glint of the sun that once warmed the Lekki horizon that I so wished to be a part of was now outside my window. I have obeyed the call of the skies.

My life had not always been one to be envied, as I used to be on the other side of the divide. I grew up in the underwater world of Makoko, better known as the Makoko-Iwaya Waterfront. I asked my mother what it was like on the day I was born, and she told me I came to the world on *orie* day of the Igbo calendar. 'My daughter, you slipped out with wealth and good charm into the waiting arms of Mama Jamal.' Her stories transported me to the morning in June when, in spite of the pain that seared through her spine, she climbed down the wooden stairs to meet Mama Jamal, the midwife who worked in the smoking compartments, sold fresh fish by day, and brought forth babies at night. Seeing my mother in distress, she immediately sprinkled water and doused the embers in the huge tins. Then, she removed her bloodied apron and washed her arms and legs at the bank of the water, all the while muttering prayers in Arabic. Mama Jamal, ready and eager, led my mother into her chambers. She spread a clean wrapper on the floors and supported my mother to her knees. My mother groaned in rhythm to the anguish that spliced through her in streams of liquid force, rising in tempo with each breath. She cursed out loud, but the older woman stuffed a piece of fabric into her mouth.

'Shhhhhh, no evil word should escape your mouth. Bear the pain of childbirth and receive your reward in your arms.' My mother bit down hard on the fabric, as hard as she desired to sink her teeth into the shoulder of the man who loved and left her.

To make her words stay with me, I build stories around the day I was born. Our home was a *face-me-I-face-you* built on wooden stilts. I woke up every morning to the chaos of half-naked children stomping playfully on the wooden verandahs. I attended the communal floating school, a two-storied solar-powered wooden structure secured on a bed of plastic barrels. I took rides on boats that had names like Benjamin and Gbenou Nu, that belonged to canoe boys who could not afford to go to school. I clutched my books to my chest as the boats glided on the still water and the acrid smell of smoked fish on charred drums chased after us. After the early morning rush, the canoe boys rented their canoes to the fishermen while they waited till midday, when the fishermen offloaded their nets bursting with fish, to tout for passengers. As I sat in my classroom and recited the multiplication table or took dictations from Mrs Kayode, I saw the canoe boys squatting in a circle under the bridge, dealing *Whot* cards and gambling their rubber bands for *kokoro* sticks. And when they slept, their chins tucked into their chests, their faces brimmed with innocence.

After school, Jamal's *Benjamin* took me to the shore where I spent the afternoon watching my mother as she climbed up and down the wooden stilts with her ladder. She spent her mornings and afternoons dredging the sands on the coast of Makoko. She would go into the depths of the lagoon armed with a bucket and her will to live. I watched her submerge into the depth of the water and then, like one baptized, emerge, grimy but victorious, with a bucketful of sand. Other labourers waited with their shovels, piling heaps of sand into boats. Others offloaded the sand into trucks, to be delivered to building sites across the city.

Our lives remained like this until my eighth birthday a year later when big-bellied government officials came with big promises of compensation and a seven-day quit notice to boot. I remember my mother cheering with her neighbours at the government's promises which only got better and better with each sentence:

'We will make life better for you!'

'The project will be completed in no time!'

A few days later, armed men sent by the same government officials ambushed us in our sleep. They came pouring into our homes like an army of soldier ants, kicking and pushing and squashing. There was shouting and gripping all around and the walls around me buckled under the weight of sledgehammers. The soldiers restrained the women and girls scampering around the narrow corridors, grabbing them by the chest as if to save them from the murky waters underneath. Our neighbours struggled to pull out bits and pieces from the rubble strewn around like pieces of Lego, and on the mainland bridge above our homes, the traffic zoomed on, unfazed. The reality of our lives soon became unanswered questions. The government promised to make our homes better so that we could have better lives. Like many others, my mother was hopeful and ready to stumble out of the familiar darkness of the slums she had lived in all her life. It soon became clear that there was no place for us to live. We had been abandoned by the government and stripped of our belongings under the watch of the men who were supposed to protect us.

The newsmen flashed our faces on national television, and it caught the attention of the Civil Liberties Organization and a few well-meaning citizens. They took some of us to Ikota, others to Epe and Jakande, but our new homes were the same. We lived in the echoes of divided lives and walked around the ghoulish stench that surrounded us. Our dignity had been wounded and shredded and trampled on. I remember watching a boy being followed by a small crowd of his peers. He was holding a stick with a dead snake wrapped around it and chanting a beggar's song. Behind the boys was Tsintsin. She was the brightest girl in my class, and now she was standing in a corner with a man. She wore a sports bra, and her hard breasts puckered and strained underneath the fabric. The man was laughing and swinging her arm. As if to confirm our doomed existence, we heard that our landlord's daughter was raped and the owner of the popular California Cinema was beaten by the armed men until his seventy-year-old body could not take it anymore. They had tried to go back to Makoko after we were asked to evacuate. And so, for the days that we remained in Ikota, our feet never left. Our kerosene lanterns punctured the darkness outside, and within our houses, the shadows of emptiness haunted us.

Growing up with a single mum had not been easy, but it was a part of my life. Emptiness is a descendant of reality, and I thought often of my never owning, or being owned. Thankfully, I am no longer searching because of the stories my mother told me. Sometimes stories can frighten us and make us not to act on our desires. But my mother was not one to let fear stop her. She had acted on her desire the day I saw her lying in her bed with a stranger. After five months in Ikota, we moved on to Kuramo Beach, by the ghettos of highbrow Lekki Peninsula. My mother had met a painter from Durban in South Africa, the same way she had met and charmed my father. My mother's lover, Kola, was a painter and photographer, and when he saw my mother the night he came to Ikota to take photographs of us for his gallery, he promised to take us with him.

His lounge, located on Beach Gate Road along Kuramo beach, was a makeshift structure constructed with wood and thatch and belonged to the wealthy proprietors who also owned bars that sold assorted drinks and food. There you would find lawyers, doctors, and artisans coming to engage the services of the red district ladies for a fee. Yet, in the confusion of it all, my mother had an eye on me and would not let me go past Jakande Second Gate like other children who went as far as Lekki Beach to get customers for their mothers.

My mother, who would not tell me who my father was, made me call Kola dad. My mother, who had slapped me flush in the face when I gaped at the mounds of her breasts, now allowed me into the room when Kola was on top of her. My mother, who always bit her lower lip firmly as she tied my wrapper across my breasts, did not know when my first blood came. My mother, who would pay fifty naira in change and wait for me as I disappeared through the hanging grass that led to restrooms on the beach, did not know that I had watched the military execution of armed robbers on television. My mother, who mercilessly cursed and beat up one of the many voyeurs that prowled around the corners of our shanty, crouching and watching through the windows as couples went in and out of the rooms, did not know that I spent many afternoons after school prowling the bar where she sold food to make up money for our weekly rent after Kola left her. I would sit on the wooden promenade and watch as couples went into the many rooms lined up on both sides of the narrow corridor. Our new space was not like the one we occupied with Kola. This room was no more than six feet five and it barely fitted either of us. It was a bare square of living space, except for a small bed and a ceiling fan that whirled noisily above as if counting each second of our lives.

It was not unusual for my mother to have visitors over after Kola left. She would send me away to Mama Rufus when she did. One night, things turned out differently. For one, I was suspicious of the stranger as soon as he came in with my mother. I detested his smiles and roving hands. When my mother went to the next lounge to primp herself, he grabbed me from behind, and as my rear bumped against his groin, I felt him harden against my skin. I struggled to pull free before my mother's sudden entrance startled him. He let go of me, and I fell forward, upsetting my mother's stacked food coolers. She was livid and deaf to her client's pleas. She pulled my ears until tears welled up in my eyes. She pulled and pulled until I was forced to bend before she pushed me outside. I whimpered, more from the hunger that gnawed at my insides than from my mother's judgment of the stranger's licentiousness as the picayune nature of men. None of the people in the other lounges appeared interested in me as I cried in front of the narrow corridor. They sauntered past me with wraps of *suya* and bottles of drinks.

Left alone, I sat still on the promenade and listened to the waves of the ocean wash back and forth. In the moonlit night, I looked out over the bare, scrubby stretch of land which had been cleared to accommodate lounges that sprang up each day. I peered into the mass of bushes and the crude pathways that snaked beyond the stars, mysterious and impenetrable, those paths along which I so often daydreamed to travel away from the life that was mine, the broad bosomed ocean, blue as the sky, foamy white as the clouds beyond the peninsula, fading into the mist beyond the roar of turbulent waters.

It took some time before the face of Madam Gabby, standing squarely in front of me, startled me to the present. She stood solidly in front of me, fondling her *babushka*. She was the proprietress who owned one of the many lounges.

'*Lady, wetin you de do outside?*'

'I . . . my mother has a visitor, ma.' I felt tears rush to my eyes.

'*Why you dey cry na? When you suppose dey happy say money go come?*'

'*I never chop ma.*'

The proprietress scoffed and told me to climb down the stairs and find somewhere else to stay, muttering something about me bringing *bad market*. She pulled me up by my arm and dragged me to a corner at the foot of the stairs. I slept off after winning the battle with my stomach that growled and droned in the dead of the night. In the meantime, my mother's client would eat up the porridge my mother made, drinking and belching foul *burukutu* breath from the illicit gin that women peddled on the beach.

I woke up to the unusual sounds coming from my mother's lounge above me. At first, it sounded like hysterical shrieks, and I sprang from the floor. Someone had draped a cloth over me; I shrugged it off and tiptoed up the stairs. When I got to our door, I opened it and crouched on the floor, peering underneath the curtains. I tried to remember where I had kept the pestle after pounding the peppers for last night's meal in case I needed it. I was still thinking about my weapon of defence when I heard my mother's laughter in the dim room.

I paused, willing the erratic beating of my heart to stop so that my mind could think. Then I looked again into the shadows as the pair on the bed rose and fell in rhythm, my mother's moans encouraged by the stranger's swift thrusts. A while later, they fell back and lay inert, breaths high, rising and falling in rhythm to the waves of the Kuramo beach.

I am drenched in sweat. I have fallen asleep with the folds of taffeta draped across my laps. It happens all the time. If I let myself, I fall back into thoughts about my childhood. I tighten my grip on my bed sheet and stare into the space of my living room. My heart hammers up to my ears, and I shut my eyes to dispel the rush of the ocean waves that crash in my head. The visions come today, as always. But if I do nothing, they remain dreams.

This time, I remember. I allow myself into the hollow of my thoughts, to the wake of the dew-covered morning, many years ago, when I had made up my mind and dared towards the ocean in my favourite print dress. I let myself quietly out of the house and ran out as fast as my naked feet could bear, splashing into the water and allowing the tides slap at my feet as the sands pulled quickly away from beneath me. I tried to stop myself from slipping into the currents, curling my toes and trying to grasp the powdered soil that pulled me swiftly into the water. In the split second before I sank in, I felt the blind stinging bolt of a head-on collision that hit me. My eyes, swollen and raw, refused to shut against the sting of the water that thrashed at my face, and my head filled up with water. I tried to hold on to the wall that imprisoned me, but I sank deeper into the belly of the sea. I thought of my mother at that moment and my tears blinded me.

I get up and clean myself in the bathroom before walking to my dresser. I stare at my reflection in the mirror and marvel at how the incandescent bulbs reflect a surreal silhouette of my lean, chiselled features. I turn each cheek sideways and run my fingers up and down the grooves of my neck. I take deep breaths and will myself to fight back the flashes of memory. My fingers slide down to my breasts and further down to my belly before descending to caress bottles of fragrances, frequent gifts from my recent regulars. Egyptian Musk. African Fantasy. Asian White Tea. Caribbean Coconut. Blue Nile. Japanese Cherry Blossom.

My fingers stay on an exquisite sylphlike decanter, *Intoxication*. I pick up the delicate crystal bottle and open the stopper with a plop before applying it on the nape of my neck, the crook of my wrists, and in-between my breasts.

I am meeting with Engineer Madumere, a pudgy man who always wears odd-coloured safari suits. After the Technology Summit I attended with him at the Liberty Hall the day before, he requested I accompany him to The Terrace. He is having a get-together for his daughter who has just graduated summa cum laude from UCLA. He wants me to meet her, and maybe when I do, I will think over his proposal for me to leave the escort agency and go back to school. 'Not in Nigeria, of course,' he had quickly added and scoffed sanctimoniously. 'Not with the incessant strikes and sexual harassment charges. I won't dare, oh gosh no.' His hand remained on the small of my back as he told me how he wanted a better life for me, away from the pretence that was my job. I gave him a stiff smile, and he bowed flirtatiously, his eyes on me. For the rest of the night, he did not let me out of his sight, and all the time he held my hand in the sleek cusps of his palms. I felt small in front of this mountain that was now my lot. He had on many occasions shown me pictures of his three daughters, all studying at prestigious universities around the world. He laughed, mostly alone, and boasted about how his daughters were more than ten sons rolled in one, and I spent our nights together feeling odd pity for his insincerity.

My doorbell is chiming, and it brings me back from my thoughts. I look at the wall clock, 7.55 p.m. I get up and pull the curtains. My handler, Kriss, is on time as always. His Toyota Camry is parked at the usual spot. He is Beninese—bleached skin, slick gold chains, canvas shoes and all—a consummate predator that lives off the lifeblood of workers like me. Everyone dreads him, especially with the rumour making the rounds that he has 'cooked' himself in some very potent herbs and always wears talismans around his waist. I suspect he fortified himself with the special charms from Marche des Feticheurs that make it impossible for the police to nail him for running a prostitution and drug peddling ring. Instead, the police work for him. They beat us and put us into empty oil drums and chase us down the alleys if we try to make an extra naira for ourselves.

'You will not wear that dress,' he says as he enters.

I ignore him and stand next to the fridge humming at my bedside. He goes to my dressing table and picks up a plastic rattail comb before turning to walk towards me. He is fondling the comb and smiling. The tension in my body cascades in quick swoops. I brace myself and straighten as he approaches. I know what he wants as he stands, breath for breath, in front of me. I keep my eyes steady on him and pull down the zipper of my sequined gown.

'All of it, lady,' he cautions.

The gown slides down my hips to the floor and lands in a pool around my legs. I take off my underwear before he asks. He walks round me, lifting my hair with the comb and pointing to parts of my body he wants to see well.

'Are we done?' I ask stiffly.

'Haha, yes, get dressed.'

I bend down and gather my clothes. The day has ended well.

I love that I am an escort. I love the new clothes and shoes and bags I get each week. I love to sit with them on the bed, fondling the intricate designs on the mini gowns, crop tops, bum shorts. I check the designer labels on the clothes and feel raw satisfaction.

'Remember that I was supposed to be off this week,' I say to Kriss as I pick up my purse from the nightstand and walk towards the door.

'You'll have to make do with the extra cash' is the gruff reply.

I smile quietly and walk to the car at an obsequious pace behind him. We have our fair share of friendship; we understand each other and know what the other wants. But I cannot have it any other way. When I had been helpless, Kriss came to my rescue, and he built for me the dependency I now have on him. He protects me from the streets, from being one of those girls that end up harassed or kidnapped or shot dead. He pays me enough for my work. He is the only one who saves me from the debris of ocean waste that was once my home.

HOMEWARD

Ken Lipenga Jr

Returning home had not been my plan, but I embraced it nonetheless. Five years had passed. Hardly enough time for people to miss me. But forget that, I was returning home. That was all that mattered. I gazed out the window, trying to convince myself there was something familiar in the variegated green geometrical patterns of the maize fields below. Maize. Perhaps there was something positive to look forward to. Something that echoed faintly from down the corridors of memories of flavour. The sweet taste of *mondokwa*, fresh maize roasted on an open flame. I could not believe I had not tasted roasted maize for the past five years. I had a cousin who was gifted with an almost otherworldly skill at roasting maize, with an uncanny ability to not char the corn as he turned it on the fire. He would carry a brazier and charcoal to a busy road junction in town and earn a bit of cash selling roast maize to passers-by on their way from work, until the government banned the selling of roast maize due to the widespread theft of maize from people's fields. I wondered if my cousin was still around, still alive, still roasting maize.

We had broken out of the clouds a few minutes earlier, and I could tell the plane was slowly descending. There had been a bit of turbulence, which made me think of the potholes plaguing the roads back home. Like mondokwa, potholes were commonplace on the roads back home, the few that were tarmacked.

Next to me, Judah was asleep, snoring softly. Like the rest of us on the plane, he did not have any immediate plans for when we arrived home. He had family in the country who would happily welcome him. Beyond that, however, he would give himself over to fate. That is our lot, he had said.

It had been a rather gruelling two weeks at Lindela. Surviving on a single, cold unappetizing meal a day. Being the subject of gawking crowds staring at us through the double-layered barbed-wire fence. As though they were the ones imprisoned. But finally, we were going home, having been declared 'aliens'. It was, the more I thought about it, a fitting word. The crowds outside would study us as though we were a different species. On the day before our departure, Judah and I were seated on a bench near the barbed barricade of the 'Repatriation Unit', just another label for the deportation centre. We knew we both stank horribly, but I could no longer perceive the odour. I was reminded of it by the odd fly that would flit by, trying to find purchase on our bodies. We waved them away subconsciously like dogs with wounded ears. But unlike the dogs, our wounds were mainly internal. And only we knew of our private hurts, of the agony we felt at being reminded that we did not belong. Of the memories of being picked in a crowd, hustled into a police van, and carted to the deportation centre like cattle to the slaughter. On that hot afternoon, I did not mind Judah sitting next to me. He was the closest thing to a friend in those circumstances. I felt a unique sort of kinship with him.

Judah had told me his story a couple of days ago. He had been involved in a fight at one of the local shebeens. Over a woman. On that particular evening, he told me, he had made two fatal mistakes. The first was to go drinking alone. This he had done due to the strong, irrational need for a woman. 'It is something you can never fully explain, especially to a woman, you know.' He looked me in the eye as he spoke, conveying what I took as a profound need to be agreed with. I nodded. 'I had money. I should have been happy. But I felt the need. I just had to fuck. I'd want to blame the devil, but that would be unfair. It was all me, man.' He said he knew if he took his friends along, his money would have been spent on alcohol, and none would be left to pay for a woman's exclusive services. So he snuck off to the shebeen alone, knowing very well that his usual drinking partners would not be there, this being January when money was tight.

It was still light outside when he arrived. He loved this time of the year. Even as late as 8 p.m., one could be assured that people would still be out and about in the streets of Khayelitsha. And this being summer, the young ladies would be in the streets, clad in extremely revealing clothes. Thigh-high skirts and body-hugging vests. Bodysuits that accentuated curves and valleys of temptation. There were a number of these women at the shebeen. For a long time, AmaJolies had been the drinking joint of choice for many in the area. And sure enough, Thembi was there. She had been his target, all along. He was not aiming for just any woman.

When he stepped through the tattered bead curtain that served as the entrance to the drinking hall, she was sitting alone, sipping a Savannah Dry. His eyes were immediately drawn to her fingers. She held the bottle with thumb and finger alone. Thumb and finger with long fingernails painted in the colours of the national flag. Thumb and finger each encircled with golden, intricately patterned rings. 'This must be how upmarket ladies hold their drinks', Judah thought. To him, Thembi's lackadaisical handling of the drink was a gesture that said, 'I can afford more of these and could drop this drink if I wanted to, but I won't'. She was alone, almost as though she had been waiting for him. She did not see him at first. He quickly procured an Amstel and found a place in a secluded corner, far from the blasting speakers, which gave him a moment to drink in the sight of her figure. It never ceased to astound him. To put it plainly, Thembi was a fat woman, no doubt. But, unlike most of the other women who frequented this place, Thembi had her fat in all the right places. Judah did not know how she maintained that figure, but he was glad she did. It was something he enjoyed looking at when he came to AmaJolies. And at night, when he woke from alcohol-induced sleep, he enjoyed visualising what he could do to that body if ever given a chance.

This evening, Thembi was wearing a dress, a bit unusual for her but pleasing to the eye nonetheless. This meant that her legs were exposed a bit more than usual, that light brown, creamy complexion that most Xhosa women laid claim to. Many a night, Judah had thought of caressing those thighs; he wondered if the caramel colour would remain on his fingertips if he ever did so, like molten milk chocolate.

Thembi gave him the occasional smile, nothing more. In the past, no matter how much alcohol he took, he never gathered enough courage to talk to her. Part of the reason was that his friends spoke of her in the vilest of terms once they had had a few. Judah remembered one particular rant. A fellow called PiDo tried his luck with the woman. He had applied the usual formula that guys used to secure a fuck, plying her with drink after drink. Savannahs had been bought by the crate, and PiDo had bragged that he was in for an exciting time that night. Unfortunately, the formula did not work. Thembi had disappeared while PiDo was in the middle of jiving to the sounds of the Black Missionaries playing on the jukebox. (The shebeen almost always played South African house music. As a result, the immigrant patrons were always delighted when sounds from home were played.) Apparently, she had left with another man. From that day, PiDo joined the legion of men frustrated at Thembi. The insults were endless:

'She thinks she's a queen, that woman. She thinks her pussy is golden. Fuck her!'

'I hear she can't even fuck proper! She just lies there like a sack of potatoes.'

'That woman is death on legs. Why do you think I don't bother with her like the rest of you fools? She's surviving on antiretrovirals!'

'That's true. I heard she has all manner of ugly, weeping sores on her chest. And that's why she will only fuck in the dark.'

'Fuck that, man! Who wants to fuck a diseased whore like that? I'd rather spend my money on these other women.'

'That's true, man. Better to fuck tried and tested pussy.'

'To hell with her, man.'

'Yeah, screw that sick bitch!'

And like that, the beer would flow, spiced by such enlightening conversation. Likewise, the conversation would flow, tongues loosened by the stream of liquor pouring down lustful throats, and the money hard-earned during the day would also flow as the men shared tales of home, stories of racism, and lies about women. Judah would remain silent through all of it. Getting drunk but never chipping in. It was entertainment, but it kept him from the woman he desired.

That was part of the reason he was there alone tonight.

Thembi saw him and flashed him that usual smile. Normally he would flash one in return and walk past to join his usual crew. But tonight he was a man with a mission. He took a swig of the Amstel and went directly to where she was sitting. He planted himself confidently next to her. The smile on her face was joined by an upraised eyebrow—slightly dyed pink and tweezed, a perfect arch if ever there was one—an expression of surprise at Judah's daring deviation from the usual script.

'Hello—' Was it a question, a greeting? Judah was not sure. In any case, his focus was on the voice. A husky, sexy, heavily accented voice that would have belonged more in a bigger woman's body. It was a voice he could not get tired of listening to, no matter how mundane the subject of conversation might be. She had spoken English to him, knowing him to be a foreigner.

'Kunjani.' Judah lilted his tongue just right, wanting to get the accurate pronunciation of the common Xhosa greeting. He did not want this lovely woman to think he was out to murder her language. It was a bold gambit, but it paid off. Thembi laughed softly at the greeting, giving Judah a glimpse of her teeth. There was a gap in the middle of the upper front row. Most people found such gaps sexy. To Judah, it did not really make a difference. He found the entire person alluring, and her dentition did not add or subtract from that.

Back when he had only been three months old in this new country, Judah had been waylaid by a couple of teenagers. He had been walking home from work, not really paying attention to his surroundings, composing a text to his brother back home, telling him that although life was difficult, he was beginning to make ends meet. This had been the routine since he found a job at a clothing factory, toiling from 6 a.m. until 5 p.m. when the factories disgorged the mainly immigrant workers from their gates, leaving them to make their way back to the townships. Six young boys had surrounded him as he walked. 'Cell phone, *wena*,' one of them hissed. Back home, his voice alone would have been enough to scare them away. But these young men obviously did not behave like the young men back home. He had been warned by his colleagues to always be on his guard, but somehow, he never thought such a thing would happen to him. He had hesitated in giving them his cell phone, and in a flash, they had their knives out. The short blades glinted in the diminishing sunlight.

He handed over the cell phone, a touchscreen Samsung. Then he watched as they turned and walked ahead of him, a bunch of teenagers who could have been returning from a football game, or a late class at school, or even from bible study. He watched them till they disappeared into a side street. Later, still shivering from the memory of the experience, he narrated the ordeal to his colleagues. They told him he had done the right thing. They even bought him a few Amstel dumpies to make him forget the experience. Then, with the alcohol loosening tongues, they reminisced about the home country, with its sweet maize and sweeter women. They agreed that Xhosa men were cowards. They never fought fair.

'They never fight fair.' That was the one thought that crossed Judah's mind as the slim fellow danced around in front of him, tossing his blade from one hand to the other. The centre of the shebeen had been turned into a battleground. The other drinkers had formed themselves into a circle around Judah and Slim, who was rattling off even louder in a superfast township Xhosa dialect. Judah could not catch much of what the fellow was saying. However, he could tell from his gestures that Slim's anger had boiled down to not tolerating disrespect from foreigners. One word that kept springing from Slim's lips, together with flecks of spit, was *kwerekwere*. Most immigrants were well acquainted with that dreaded word. It meant that one did not belong, that one was not worthy to be in the same space as the speaker, breathing the same air as them, much less drinking the same beer and fucking the same women. It was a word of unity and a word of disunity. It unified Malawians, Zimbabweans and Mozambicans in their otherness. It disunited other Africans from black South Africans.

The situation had escalated quickly. One minute he was talking to Thembi, savouring the sound of her laugh, the radiance of her teeth, the sweaty fragrance of *woman* that wafted from her. He even got to touch the alluring thumb and finger that had coursed through his dreams many a time, teasing him with possibilities. He had never thought he could make her laugh, yet here it was, happening. A part of him regretted the fact that his homeboys were not around to witness his moment of conquest. What did he say to make her laugh? He could not remember. She told him she found his pronunciation of Xhosa words fascinating. She said it made the language sound fresh. So focused was he on the woman, wanting to catch every millisecond of her movements, every word she said, that he was oblivious to the glares from many of the men in the shebeen.

The next minute, he was confronted by Slim, an angry young man telling him, in a township patois that blended Xhosa and English, that he was being disrespectful. It had not even taken any knowledge of martial arts for Judah to know he could take on the young drunken fellow. For Slim, the fight was going to be a performance, a chance to put the kwerekwere in his place, to remind him to respect his hosts. From there, events escalated quickly.

Judah would never know why the police had appeared on the scene. Perhaps they were simply patrolling the location, looking for troublemakers. Perhaps they had been tipped by someone. Or maybe they were simply looking for a drink. He would not know. He hated the fact that he did not even have time to savour the short victory over Slim. When the two plump policemen walked into the shebeen, Judah had been standing over Slim, who was moaning in pain on the floor, grabbing his left arm sleeve, totally soaked in blood.

Thembi had long since disappeared from the scene.

Looking back, Judah realized that was the moment his trip home began. He and his homeboys had often talked about returning home, with a nostalgia that was always short-lived. A week never went by without something happening to remind them of home. It could be political events back home, such as the recent elections and the usual accusations of rigging. It might be one's encounter with thugs in the township, which would inevitably lead to discussions, over a few glasses of Amstel, of the incredible levels of crime in their adopted country. In some cases, it would be experiences of xenophobia and racism which made them remember home. Such conversations would always end the same way: 'We've been here too long, guys. It's time to go home.'

And they would all agree. Until the next pay cheque arrived or until the next Xhosa woman smiled at them, upon which the homesickness would fade away, and Khayelitsha would begin to feel like home again. In those moments, they would forget their complaints and instead pat each other on the back for their endurance, the fact that they were true men for managing to survive in a country that was not theirs. The conversations would still be about home, but this time, they would be complaints about the people back home who, like young nestlings with their mouths open, would be forever expectant, waiting for the *mtchona* outside the country to send them rands. Then someone would chip in the fact that the home country was crippled by poverty and that to return home would be to enter a wilderness of joblessness and misery.

'My mother is surviving on the little that I am able to send her from here. If I should return home, with no job, who will support her?'

In this light, the racism would slowly become more tolerable. After all, racist remarks did not draw blood. And if one looked closely, they would reason, the xenophobia was only practised by a few misguided folks. The rest were friendly and welcoming. After all, wasn't it just last week that Cosmas married a Xhosa woman? This could indeed become home, as long as one was willing to work hard. It was not a country for softies. They needed to be thankful that they were here, in the land of opportunity, instead of back home wallowing in poverty.

The plane touched down. We were quickly processed through immigration at the airport, with the immigration officials making snide remarks about our return. They offered us exorbitant exchange rates for the few rands we had. We had little choice. Finally outside, for want of something to say, I again asked Judah what his plans were.

'I had time to think, during the flight. I have decided on what to do. I need to find a Malawian woman, then a hot meal, some money, then book the next Munorurama back to where I belong, wena.'

THE AUTHORS

Athol Williams is renowned for his literary and advocacy work to foster a more just society. He has published sixteen books, including six books of poetry. His most recent book, Whistleblowing (Geko, 2021) stems from his ordeal following blowing the whistle on state capture and corruption in South Africa. He is a two-time winner of the Sol Plaatje European Union Poetry Award as well as four other literary awards. Over 100 of his poems have been published in journals and anthologies around the world. He is a regular speaker and author of articles relating to social and ethical issues. Athol holds six degrees from Harvard, Oxford, MIT, LSE, London Business School and Wits. www.atholwilliams.com

Joshua Chizoma is a Nigerian writer. His works have been published or forthcoming in Prairie Schooner, AFREADA, Entropy Magazine, Kalahari Review, Prachya Review, and elsewhere. His story, "A House Called Joy" won the 2018 Kreative Diadem Prize in the Flash fiction category. He was shortlisted for the 2021 Afritondo Short Story Prize and won the 2020 Awele Creative Trust Short Story Prize. He is an alumnus of the 2019 Purple Hibiscus Creative Writing Workshop taught by Chimamanda Adichie.

Desta Haile is a British-Eritrean writer, vocalist, and educator. She holds an MA in Black British Writing from Goldsmiths, University of London and is currently Deputy Director of the Royal African Society. In her free time she runs Languages through Music and Sisters Only Language Summit. Ethio-Cubano is her second short story, and the first one to be published in physical form.

Rémy Ngamije is a Rwandan-born Namibian writer and

photographer. He is the founder and chairperson of Doek, an independent arts organisation in Namibia supporting the literary arts. He is also the co-founder and editor-in-chief of Doek! Literary Magazine. His debut novel The Eternal Audience Of One is forthcoming from Scout Press (S&S). His work has appeared in The Johannesburg Review of Books, American Chordata, Lolwe, and Granta, among others. He won the Africa Regional Prize of the 2021 Commonwealth Short Story Prize. He was shortlisted for the AKO Caine Prize for African Writing in 2020 and 2021 and was also longlisted and shortlisted for the 2020 and 2021 Afritondo Short Story Prizes respectively

Faraaz Mahomed is a researcher and practitioner in the field of mental health and human rights. His short stories and travel writing have appeared in Granta, the Sunday Times, the Georgia Review and others. In 2016, Faraaz won the Commonwealth Short Story Prize for the African Region. In 2020, his stories were longlisted for the Bristol Prize and the Boston Review Short Story Prize. Also in 2020, he was runner up in the inaugural Toyin Falola African literature prize and in the Superlative Short Story contest. He is currently working on a novel.

Yop Dalyop is a seventeen-year-old Nigerian writer who likes to explore societal issues with fiction. She has published articles highlighting positivity and runs awareness programmes for children. When she isn't learning French, Yop enjoys exploring Abuja street food, bookshops and watching movies with her siblings. She is always looking for opportunities to share and improve her writing.

Henry Kabubu Mutua is a writer from Machakos, Kenya. He is currently an undergraduate student of computer science at the Jomo Kenyatta University of Agriculture and Technology. He is working on a novel. Find him on Twitter @kabubumutua or on Instagram @kabubumutua or his website henrymutua.com

Justin Clement, also known as Haku Jackson, is a storytelling artist whose works explores the meanings and methods of life. His works have been listed for various prizes and awards, including the African Writers Award, The Awele Creative Trust Award, and some others. He's an alumnus of the Purple Hibiscus Trust Creative Writing Workshop, by Chimamanda Adichie, and he's also the recipient of the 2020 Gulliver Travel Grant awarded by the Speculative Literature Foundation. His fiction appears in the young adult anthology, Water Birds on the Lakeshore, and he currently writes for the digital comics company, Comic Republic. He's an admirer of cats and other talking animals.

Chidera Nwume is a student of Mass Communication at the Pan Atlantic University, Lagos. She is a writer, baker, plant mum, and serial daydreamer. She hopes to pursue writing as a professional career.

Dennis Mugaa is a writer from Meru, Kenya. He has been a Black Warrior Review Fiction Contest finalist and an Ebedi-fellow. His work has appeared or is forthcoming in *Jalada*, *Lolwe* and *Washington Square Review.*

Prosper Wilton Makara is a research technician at the National Biotechnology Authority in Zimbabwe. You are most likely to find him curled up in bed reading books by Chimamanda Adichie and Tsitsi Dangarembga. His body of work is diverse and heavily influenced by the above-named writers and Warsan Shire's poetry among other talented African writers.

Debbie Vuha lives in Accra, Ghana. She likes to draw and write stories, and isn't very good at talking about herself, which explains the length of this bio.

Ngansop A. Roy is a Cameroonian engineer and writer living in the U.A.E. His short fiction has appeared or is forthcoming in The Shallow Tales Review, the Kalahari Review, and the NaiWA 2021 Anthology. He is a Nairobi Writing Academy scholar.

Charlie Muhumuza is a writer and lawyer living in Kampala. His short fiction has been published in Isele magazine, Jalada Africa, Ibua journal and elsewhere. Charlie was awarded third prize at the inaugural Kalahari Short Story Competition in 2020 and was longlisted for the 2021 Afritondo Short Story Prize.

Queen Nneoma Kanu is a PhD student at the University of Louisiana at Lafayette, USA. She obtained her Bachelor's and Master's degrees in English (Arts) from the University of Lagos, Nigeria, and teaches African literature at Federal University, Wukari, Taraba State, Nigeria.

Ken Junior Lipenga teaches English Literature at the University of Malawi. He holds an MA in Literature from the University of Malawi and a PhD in Literature from Stellenbosch University, South Africa. He likes reading works of African literature and writing critiques about them. When he is not conducting research for academic papers, he writes fiction and poetry.

An anthology of love stories from Africa

Yellow means stay
An anthology of love stories from Africa

Yellow Means Stay is a collection of enthralling love stories from across Africa and the black diaspora. The stories are a dynamic blend of the poetic and narrative, the spousal and familial, the suggestive and explicit, the dramatic and measured, the straight and queer, the sad and humorous, the past and future, life and after life.

"... these stories of connection, intimacy and lust are a delicious read."
—Megan Ross, Author of Milk Fever

The Institute for Creative Dying

On the slopes of Northcliff Ridge, below the second-highest vantage point in Johannesburg, ladybugs get ravaged by ants, ants are zombified by fungi, and fungi become the means for awakening. Above these stand an unnumbered house, protected by high walls and obscured by tall trees. Here five strangers meet, all of them yearning for a way through to the end of life as they have known it.

The Institute for Creative Dying is a colourful examination of human mortality amid botanical, technological, and animalic worlds. It is a story that explores the limits of living. One that asks whether it is possible to die before your death.

9 781838 027926